HITLER'S

GIRLS

HITLER'S
GIRLS

A NOVEL

EMMA TENNANT

& HILARY BAILEY

OR Books

New York · London

Published by OR Books, New York and London
Visit our website at www.orbooks.com

First printing 2013

Cataloging-in-Publication data is available from the Library of Congress.
A catalog record for this book is available from the British Library.

ISBN 978-1-939293-31-2 paperback
ISBN 978-1-939293-32-9 e-book

This book is set in Century. Typeset by Lapiz Digital, Chennai, India.
Printed by BookMobile in the United States and CPI Books Ltd in the
United Kingdom.

EDITOR'S NOTE

St Ronan's (the name is changed, to protect the woman who lived and suffered there long enough to expiate the gravest of sins) is an island off the coast of Scotland, in the Western Hebrides.

There is just one house on the island. The house is white, boasts fourteen rooms, and was built circa 1840. On the top story are bow windows. Behind them, day after day of her interminable incarceration, the lone resident of St Ronan's House looked out to sea. She was awaiting, perhaps, the return of a lover or a child. It would be simple to add that she went mad—or that the storms were particularly Gothic in that part of the ocean near the great rounded hills of the island of Mull.

But it was not so. Curlews and seagulls did, it is true, make their calls. A lone boatman added to the sense of isolation, when he rowed in with provisions—these collected by the housekeeper, Mrs. Nairn. Otherwise, existence was pleasant enough, on St Ronan's, the sunny aspect of the island being enhanced by the beaches, which are uniformly covered with minuscule shells so yellow they could be mistaken, from the distant upper windows of the house, for fields of buttercups.

At the time of her disappearance, people on the mainland had long ago ceased expressing their curiosity about the mysterious inhabitant of St Ronan's. The house, only a sliver visible from the sea, was on occasion pointed out to groups of trippers on seal-watching expeditions in the fishing vessels hired out at Oban. Mrs. Nairn, when she was later to be questioned on the possible identity of the person or persons who assisted her charge to leave the island, avowed there had not been a single visitor to the place since as far back as she could remember.

She—and her mother before her—had been at St Ronan's since a few months after the outbreak of the Second World War.

The enquiry into the escape—if such is the word—of the lady of St Ronan's was soon dropped, for lack of evidence. Though it goes without saying that this mythical figure has by now been seen at least as often as Lord Lucan: in Brazil, Bavaria and even, more locally, on the Hebridean island of Barra.

Mrs. Nairn swears she knows nothing. Only her great-nephew Tam, over on the island for a day's fishing from Mull, insists he saw a very old lady one morning at dawn, walking past his room on the lower floors of St Ronan's House and making for the broken jetty down by the sea wall.

The old lady may have taken the little boat, barely seaworthy, which has lain all these years up-ended at the top of the beach. She may have tried to row herself, against a ferociously strong spring tide, to the mainland.

Locals point out that someone so arresting in appearance would, in that case, have been noticed and reported at once. Visitors point out that the absence of TV and newspapers at St Ronan's in the near sixty years since her imprisonment there would have rendered its resident incapable of dealing with the changes in modern life—while those same locals sarcastically pointed out in return that nothing very much had changed on the bare hillsides and in the sparsely furnished crofters' cottages and bothans since then.

Either way, St Ronan's House is now empty. Mrs. Nairn is rehoused with her daughter in Peebles. The disappearance of the Lady of St Ronan's has elevated her to something like the Loch Ness Monster: never actually seen, an object of fantasy, emblem of an evil, prehuman age.

WITH NANNY & HITLER

FRANCE 1936

They told me when the news came that we had just an hour to pack our things. Then Franz would drive us to the station. "Don't forget the butterfly dress," Nanny says as we run into the house, "the butterflies say 'see you next year,' don't they Clemmie . . . ? The pretty butterflies say 'be sure to behave in Germany, and you'll be back here, all of you.' Come on Clem, don't dawdle, what will Liese say if we're late?"

I can't say which of all the people gathered to see us off— people I'd hated or loved throughout the holidays—except for Nanny who went ignored, but secretly was the only one at Les Mimosas that I feared and knew I had to obey—was the most likely to stay in my memory once we'd got into the big black car and gone down the coast road in the direction of St Tropez. There was the Duchess, of course. "Look at her shoes!" Nanny said each time we had to go out in the car with the woman who looked like a man, although Hans called him Madame Le Duchesse, and there was Fräulein Baum who took me to the

5

gooseberry bushes behind the tennis court and told me I was going to meet a very important man when we got to Germany. "He might invite you to Rumpelmayer's where they have whipped cream as thick as this," and Fraulein Baum stretched her fingers wide, but all I could think of was a plate of sausages. "The English girls are happy to be invited by Herr Hitler, my new friend Puzi had said, and Clemency, darling, he would love you."

JEAN HASTIE'S NOTEBOOK

I would not have consented to come to London if it had not been for two factors. My work for the Scottish National Trust keeps me inevitably north of the Border; I last paid a fleeting visit on the occasion of the Hunt Debate (to my relief, I may add, the Trust elected to continue its ban of stag hunting. I have always considered these the most noble of animals). That the second factor in my decision to return south also involves a hunt—but, to my mind, of an infinitely more sinister nature—may give some inkling of the severity of conditions needed to lure me from a comfortable life of semi-retirement in Edinburgh. Plus, I do not hesitate to add, the extraordinary coincidence of discovering that the quarry—the victim—the subject of this outstandingly appalling murder—was none other than my childhood friend, my old companion of holiday and school.

The first information was on TV. I do not watch often, and when I do it is usually to catch the news. I long ago cancelled the meretricious sheets which pass for the newspapers of today.

Two evenings ago, as I settled with my tea in front of the set, I received the horrifying information that the woman, briefly mentioned in a morning bulletin as a "retired social worker"—recipient of upwards of ten stab wounds on the occasion of returning to her home in West London—was Monica Stirling. I recognised the street, Bandesbury Road in Kilburn. I heard, with a grimness that may well be imagined, that the murdered woman's assailants were "a girl gang." Worst of all, I ingested the additional news that the dead woman's daughter had been numbered among the assailants—and was now missing.

A further reason to come south—which, I own, may strike a frivolous note in the company of such a horror as violent death—was the fact that Monica Stirling (whom, it must be said, I have not seen for many years) had replied a couple of months back to my letter of condolence at the death of her elderly mother, aged one hundred, with a request for information on St Ronan's House, by the island of Mull. I had been working the past six months on committees, forming applications for conservation orders—and, however I may disapprove of the scheme, even going so far as to approach the Lottery Heritage Fund—in order to save the facade and structure of this unusual island house. (St Ronan's was sold by the Wilsford family last year after the disappearance of the last remaining family member.

The buyer, a Dutch businessman, went bankrupt and the island house, uninhabited as it is, was left to rot.)

That Monica Stirling should have (presumably) found the early-nineteenth-century building as worthy of refurbishment and care as my fellow members of the Trust and I found it, was moving indeed. The link with the preservation of an edifice such as St Ronan's, coupled with a sense that our childhood friendship had bred a shared love of the old, the historic, brought me to London. I stay at the Avondale Club, for Scottish University Women. It is as quiet and well run as I remember it.

I shall add here that this is the worst case I have ever known. It is scandalous that a respectable woman such as Monica should be assassinated—there is no other word for it—while her killer goes free. I am able only now to release notes, diary entries, interviews, and interrogations, regarding my tentative exploration of the inexplicably vile end of a gentle woman.

The most unpleasant shock came on arrival at Monica's West London house today. A brief visit to the police reveals they have dismissed all other suspects in the "girl gang" of which TV news made so much. They claim they need the whereabouts of only one of Monica's attackers: they wish to interview Monica's granddaughter, the child she had brought up from infancy, after the deaths of both parents. The police are looking for my goddaughter. Mel.

9

JEAN HASTIE'S DIARY

I intend to collect all I can, concerning the murder of Monica Stirling. The disappearance of Monica's fifteen-year-old grand-daughter subsequent to the brutal murder of the woman I had known as a childhood friend in the North is of course my main concern. I informed the police that I had no idea of the where-abouts of Mel.

"Leave it to us," said the young dog-faced inspector, who had just spent half an hour questioning me on my knowledge of Monica's habits (I knew virtually nothing). Finally, I had to suggest it was time to end our interview, and he appeared as relieved as I was when I went out the door.

Here I am in the neat semi in West London where Monica lived until yesterday. The house isn't as neat now as she must have kept it, of course, since the gang came in and ransacked it. What had they wanted?

11

"Money," the neighbour Mrs. Walker said after I let myself in with the key Monica sent me all those years ago in case I wanted somewhere to stay if I came South.

I never did. Now it's too late. "Five murders this year so far in Kilburn," Mrs. Walker said before I shut her out onto the suburban tiled path. "Money for drugs. That's what they want."

But I'm not so sure. I need time, to find who killed Monica Stirling. Mrs. Walker's bossy, ingratiating manner has guaranteed her a role as star witness. She claims Mel would have no qualms in killing her mother, in order to obtain this revolting drug. But I find I cannot agree with her. Mel—little Melissa Stirling—a matricide?

The street where Monica lives is long and straight. There are rowan trees planted along the pavement on both sides. In late summer they will be covered in red and orange berries— and I can't help thinking of the little town in Scotland where we grew up and went to the same school, Monica and I. I try to remember what we did to amuse ourselves, in the steep granite town where the women worked at the wool mill and the men were either unemployed or worked on land belonging to the local lairds. How did the long rainy summers and cold winters go by?

The answer is simple. I studied, for I knew I wanted to teach and to understand history.

Monica read *Woman's Own* and then looked embarrassed when she confessed to it.

Monica wanted only to get married. "Kinder, Küche, Kirche," I used to tease her, quoting the aims for women of the man who had just tried—and failed—to destroy us all and bring Europe under his control.

But Monica had no idea what I meant. She said her stars told her she would marry soon. And she did, she married Ian Stirling when she was eighteen years old and he was little more. He'd come North fruit-picking. I can see him now, standing by the raspberry canes in a sodden mac. Ian went on to work in an accountancy firm and they later relocated to London.

About that time their daughter Janet was born. After they'd tried for ages. And then, the tragedy: Janet and her husband killed in a road accident. The baby, Mel—Melissa— strapped behind them in a carrycot, alive and well. Ian and Monica, then sixty, took the baby.

I did what I could for my godchild, though evidently it wasn't enough. I didn't come South and use the key: I sent books at Christmas and a card with a note folded in it for her birthday. The notes increased from £1 to £10 as the years went by—I don't approve of older people who don't keep up with the times. Her last birthday in June I sent £20 and—though Monica dropped me a line and said Mel had been "overjoyed"—she,

Monica, thought it was too much. They didn't need money at Bandesbury Road now. And she folded the note back in the envelope to me.

I admit I was a little offended at first. Now I wonder: why did Monica send the money back to me? She'd been widowed three years and I hadn't heard that her circumstances had improved.Was she too proud to let on that her pension wasn't enough?

Or—least likely of—had she suddenly come into money? If she had, it wouldn't have been from her parents. The doctor and his wife weren't well off. Besides, they had three sons, children of their own.

Then I remembered. Monica was adopted. She'd told me when we were out in the playground of the school at break. I can see—just as clearly as I saw Ian, fingers blue from cold as he pulled fruit from the tall, prickly bushes—the time she spoke about herself and her family. A light drizzle was falling and the chimney from the mill sent up a plume of very white smoke into the sky.

Perhaps in those days the fact that the identity of the biological parents was kept permanently concealed made conjecture and wishful thinking less prevalent than they are today.

Monica showed no interest whatsoever in her true parentage. We took pandrops from a bag that was already damp from the insistent drizzle and we sucked and then crunched at the same time, which made us both burst out laughing.

To this day I never thought of the subject again.

But then I thought of Monica very little. And now everyone thinks of her: her plump face on TV, dark hair neatly set, typical suburban housewife. Murdered—another statistic for Kilburn. No close friends. Had Mel antagonised everyone round here?

I look round the house but I see nothing of value. Nothing to show that Monica had suddenly found herself heir to a fortune.

But then I wouldn't know what had been there for the taking. Monica's house had clearly been ransacked.

And I come near to smiling as I walk across the cork tiles of the kitchen (muddy still from trampling feet at the time of Saturday's crime). For it occurs to me that Monica, who loved historical romances, would have revelled in a lurid plot such as the one I had just concocted about heirs and a fortune. "What happens next, Jean?" Monica would say when we were young, her eyes wide. "What does it mean, inheritance?"

But I fear there will be no romance in this compilation of memories, records, and observations surrounding the murder of Monica Stirling. I have taken pains to assure the accuracy of the facts I present here.

And I, Jean Hastie—who am now, as it transpires, the only remaining friend of Monica Stirling, after all these years—I,

Jean, will attempt to find Monica's daughter. It is impossible to believe she killed—and robbed—her mother, and then ran away.

First, the kitchen must be thoroughly cleaned. Then the stairs, bedroom, and sitting-room of Monica's house, so she need feel no shame, even in death.

This is where she and I were alike, even when we were very young. I was tidy. I liked to organise. I kept my filing cabinet immaculate.

Monica would scrub and polish until the doctor's house on the outskirts of Eddleston shone and gleamed.

Which makes it all the odder that there are practically no cleaning agents to be found here at 109 Bandesbury Road.

Just a moth-eaten duster, an abandoned tin of furniture polish, and a half-solidified bottle of Jif.

HITLER'S DAUGHTER

My name is Clemency Wilsford. I am sixteen years old and I am English, although Nanny says I am growing more German every day. We come each summer to the house Uncle Leader has built especially for his friends. "If you are naughty," Nanny says, "Uncle Leader won't invite you any more. Putzi will not be your friend, there will be no dancing after tea in the barn." So I must be good, I must pretend that I am happy in this house in the mountains where I want to run away and die.

Uncle Leader's big friend is a woman who talks about him all the time. "Isn't the Führer wonderful," she says and when she sees me she says it in a loud whispery voice—"hasn't he marvellous eyes? Marvellous cruel eyes. . . but he's not cruel, is he Clemmie? He wants to look after you, just like Nanny does. . . he loves us all, Clemmie, and you're going to be good while we play our little game, aren't you my armes kind.*"*

What I hate most of all is the game. They played it last year at Berchtesgaden and I was told to stand in a corner and

17

not look round until Putzi called out to me to move. "It's just like a game of statues," the big woman says and I can smell her breath on my neck, so I scream. "Now halt," the big woman insists—and I look round because I know I must. But they're just where they were before. "How does the magic work?" Uncle Leader says in a funny babyish voice and they all burst out laughing. "Show us again, Magda"—and the big woman who is very chic, that is Putzi's word for her, jumps forward and right onto the thin green lawn where the grown-ups play if it isn't raining. I hate the game because I know it's for making people do something they wouldn't normally do.

But nothing is normal here. Putzi said I may never go home, and I say I don't care if I go or not, I refuse to sing the songs and say how much I love Uncle Leader. I hate playing statues too.

NOTEBOOK

I didn't like Jim Graham. The minute I laid eyes on him I felt sorry for Monica, as if she were still alive and didn't want me to know she had no-one better to spend an evening with when her teenage daughter was stuck up in her room on the phone or out making trouble with other youngsters. There is something just a little too friendly about Jim—and now, after letting me in to 119 Bandesbury Road, he's growing friendlier by the minute.

Which is odd, considering we're sitting side-by-side on a collapsed old settee in his front room and staring at a video of the murder of Monica Stirling.

I have a gin and tonic in my hand. Jim has a whisky. We might be viewing the Lord Mayor's show or horse-jumping, for all the effect the spectacle is having on Jim Graham. "I made a copy of Mrs. Walker's video-tape," Jim said to me as he let me in to the little semi which is as untidy as Monica's must in usual circumstances have been neat. "Our Neighbourhood Watch in person. You met her for a moment I believe, Mrs. Hastie?"

I won't permit this type of address. I've never been married and the assumption that the prefix Mrs. is a compliment to a single woman is, I find, deeply offensive. I corrected Mr. Graham—and couldn't help enjoying the moment of panic when he visibly couldn't decide whether "Dr." was medical or academic. As I explained that I was a part of the Edinburgh University history faculty, his eyes appeared to flicker in relief.

Monica had told me about Jim. He'd drop in on her from five doors down and they'd do the crossword together—a very useful friend, Monica's letter had said, but somehow there was a tone of desperation. Jim had been a journalist—a Foreign Correspondent, I think she described him. Retired now. A faint hint of a re-marriage vanished after the first letter and thereafter Jim was hardly referred to at all.

At the time, I thought nothing of Monica's silence on the subject of Jim. But here he is—on my little cassette recorder I take to historic houses in Scotland when I want to record the owners' descriptions of their properties and the relationship of those properties to the Scottish National Trust.

"Oh yes, Dr.—Dr. Hastie, Monica Stirling and I were very good friends. It was great to call round there—she preferred that to coming here—one can see why, I'm afraid!"

A loud, self-deprecating laugh. Jim Graham is clearly one of those bachelors who considers that his living in a pigsty must be attractive to women. Did I mention: Graham has balding dark hair and very deep-set eyes? He may have been handsome once—now he has let himself go, and so he resembles the unfortunate condition of his house and furnishings more closely perhaps than he can realise. The friendly, almost familiar manner sits ill with an inbred arrogance: Jim's look is one of superiority and self-righteousness masked by a desire to appear modern and trendy. Hence the frequent Americanisms. I have heard colleagues at the Faculty, freshly over from the USA, refer to this type of parlance as "guy."

Now Jim is speaking of Monica in what I've come to think of as his "forensic" voice. "It was the night before last. We'd agreed to meet. I went up to 109. She was great company, Monica, really great!"

I cannot say precisely why, but I had a strong feeling at this point that Monica's death, far from being a tragedy to Jim Graham, is actually providing him with some excitement. I must have looked away, because he goes on: "Don't get me wrong, Dr. Hastie! This type of thing doesn't turn me on. I was horrified to hear—I detest violence as much as any man who's been up against it all those years. Vietnam, Cambodia, Rwanda. . ."

"Mr. Graham, I have to ask you these questions because it's a long time since I last saw Monica. Fifteen years, to be precise. I was godmother to—to Janet's daughter. Mel had never been

21

christened. Monica thought it important. The christening was in Edinburgh."

"Yes, yes." Jim Graham swivels round in his chair, pressing the "pause" button on the controller at the same time. Now I feel him tensing: I'd been wrong in thinking Monica's dreadful end had been a titillation to him: it's the mention of the girl's name that gets him on the move. I conceal a smile, thinking of the time the old Laird of Melquhane had given away his knowledge of a secret hiding place for the Casket letters, all because my assistant at the time, provocatively named Mary Seton after one of the Scottish Queen's ladies-in-waiting, had come with me on the case. But I digress.

"Yes yes," Jim is saying with the perfunctory manner of a man who is trying hard to hide a lifelong lust. "Mel. . . don't you think you should look at the video now, Dr. Hastie?"

There, I had to admit, Jim Graham was right. Squeamishness, pity—whatever the mixture amounted to, I'd not been able to bring myself to witness on film the brutal murder of a woman I'd grown up with—even, in the long, lonely summers in that Borders mill town, loved. It was repulsive to me that bossy Mrs. Walker, from the recesses of her over-furnished semi, had been so cool as to take out a video camera and record the brutal death of a respectable, kind-hearted neighbour. Come to that, Jim had been quick enough to insist on copying the film. It was even more repellent to imagine that the whole of Bandesbury Road, snug with cups of tea and crumpets, were right now sitting back and watching the assault on Monica Stirling. This was a land of Crimewatch—even Jim's "virtual" grief seemed to fit in with the life-at-one-remove-ness of it all.

"There's Mel, Dr. Hastie," Jim said, pointing at the screen and placing his whisky on a little table already well-rimmed with the bases of highball glasses. "Just in case—well, if you hadn't seen her for a while, as you said. . ."

A posse of girls comes down the street—the street I recognise in the video as Bandesbury Road. The girls are like aliens. Shaved heads. Bulging muscles. Tattoos everywhere—I see a swastika, a green bug-eyed serpent, and Celtic crosses on every inch of exposed skin.

The gang increases speed and starts to close the gap on its prey. A woman in a donkey-brown coat. Big shopping bag. Shoulder bag tucked under chin and strapped across the stomach: a careful woman. Shoes are clearly pinching: she stops and moves the weight of her shopping bag from right to left hand. As she stoops, her profile is visible. Monica—older, but definitely, recognisably Monica.

Now the gang closes round her. Jim's house is in the background. Monica breaks away and runs up to her own gate. Hunted. Prey without hope of escape. Fifteen girls, tall, some

23

with chains. It's hard to realise I'm only seeing a picture now: maybe because it's here, it's right outside in the street.

"I'll rewind," Jim says in that matter-of-fact way he has. I'm convinced this ex-journalist would rewind footage from the stitching together of Frankenstein without a qualm. And I understand I'm badly thrown by the experience of watching the tape. I pray for the frozen tableau to remain like that, stable, unmoving: the only way to ensure I miss out on the actual bloody details of poor Monica's struggle and death is to concentrate on the girl.

"Yes, I wasn't sure which was Mel," I say a little over-eagerly—but Jim appears not to notice my blatant lie.

For of course I'd recognised Mel. My heart sinks to my shoes as the backwards dance of the rewind commences. Like figures in a nightmare receding, the gang races away from Monica along the dull stretch of Bandesbury Road. The girls pass a blond young man, who is staring up at a "For Sale" board outside a red, gabled house on the corner. I do indeed see Mel amongst them. She looks much as she did in the school photos Monica used to send me. She has a pudgy face, but she's prettier now than she was. Though that's not a word you'd use: her head is shaved even more closely than the other girls' and her face, neck, and shoulders are so covered with tattoos you might believe her an ancient Briton, covered in woad.

"Your goddaughter," Jim says. "With her friends Kim—
she's the Afro-Caribbean one—and Dev, the bottle blonde." He
rises and goes to the drinks tray. I find I'm shaking. I appear
to have drunk my gin and tonic. Why do I allow Jim Graham to
put his hand on the back of my neck, to take my glass from my
hand, and to fill it up? I must go now—back to Monica's house
to lock up with the key she sent me "just in case" and make my
way back to the Avondale Club.

I realise I haven't found the answer to even one question.
They've all been banished by the spectacle of Monica's murder—for, of course, Jim hasn't spared me. As I turned to take
the proffered drink, the fast forward button propelled us into
the climax of the scene. A hand on a long white arm, horribly
firm. . . gripping the knife, knuckles white with the strain. The
silent scream of the quarry, the spouting blood, the sudden dis-
persal of the gang down Bandesbury Road, leaving only a star-
tled-looking estate agent turning away from the camera, mobile
clamped to ear—calling the police, talking in short bursts into
his phone—then the switch to the BBC, the evening news. All
of this made it impossible for me to ask what I now do ask, very
urgently: "Why do the police consider Mel to have been. . . to
have been the one who killed Monica?"

Jim explains. He's back on the settee beside me, and his
knees are clamped against mine as if we are forced to endure a

ride on the seat of a bus that is too small to take both of us. "The knife, Dr. Hastie. Jean."

I knew what this former investigative journalist and Foreign Correspondent was going to say. I didn't want to hear it.

But Jim surprises me. I see he is a man of dull surprises— not unlike the crossword clues he and Monica used to pore over, word games contrived and unnecessary to life. I wait to hear his enthusiastic description of Monica's barbecues, of the casseroles made from strips of meat, of the preparation of her *boeuf en daube* (she'd written to me about that, excited all those years ago by the *cuisine* of Elizabeth David). I waited, in vain, for the amateur theatricals of the knife.

"The knife is missing. The police think it came from Monica's kitchen," Jim says briskly. "But, as you have noticed, Jean, the whole place is in a bit of a mess. Doesn't give the impression of a regular venue for—well—eating, relaxing, asking in the neighbours for a spot of chow. Wouldn't you agree?"

I take the opportunity, as the mixed image of Mel on the screen begins to jump and flicker, to rise from the sofa and demonstrate, as only the British can, that I am preparing to leave. But Jim, after his sudden lapse into Colonial lingo, pays no attention whatsoever and adjusts the video control before leaning further back in his seat. Mel is framed fully once more: she resembles a Fayoum painting of a head, impossibly distant, a representation of an unknowable woman from a pagan, forgotten shrine.

"You see, Jean, Monica hadn't been keeping her house too clean, as perhaps you perceived." I bristled here—did Jim suggest I was not one to notice gross disorder in a home? For a moment I was about to remark crossly that I had, of course, seen the gap in the arrangement of knives on the wall of Monica's kitchen. I almost informed this pompous and self-important man that the fine set of knives had been a gift from none other than myself—several Christmases back, when Monica wrote that she was thinking of taking up Chinese cooking. Had even gone so far as to buy herself a wok. Then I reflected that to boast of buying the murder weapon used on one's childhood best friend would render Jim the less crass one out of the two of us. The memory of my jovial phone call to Monica that Christmas Day brings tears to my eyes: "Now you can chop to your heart's content," I said. Why on earth did I never come to London and visit Monica when she was still alive?

Why, for that matter, had I not known she had let herself go—and the house along with her? Had she gone to pieces at the death of her mother and her husband, Ian? I began to feel sorry for Mel—until the dreadful evidence of the knife raised its blade in the mind. But was it strange that a fifteen-year-old girl would run away from a home so neglected and sad?

"Dr. Hastie!" Jim says. He uses the formal address but he makes it sound like the first move in a serious, possibly sexual attack. "There is more to all this than you think. May I suggest you come and sit down again and hear it?" And the neighbour of Monica Stirling pats the vacated sofa seat with his hand—as if, I cannot help thinking, I am a child or a pet dog. "You see, when Monica came to see me on Saturday night she was frantic with fear. I confess, I was astonished to see her at my door. She'd let her house slip—well, I put that down to grief at her bereavement, even if it was quite a while ago. Women can be affected that way when they live alone, it's a well-established fact."

I have tried to eliminate my responses to Jim Graham and his frequent offensive remarks while editing the account he gave me on the night of Monday, March 4th, the account of the last time he saw Monica Stirling. I did not, however, accept the invitation to join Mr. Graham on the settee in front of the permanently renewed image of Mel. I stood where I was, coat still in hand, by the door.

JIM'S STORY

"You won't mind if I'm frank with you, Jean.

"The sight of Monica Stirling in a housecoat was the opposite of a big treat. I want to get rid of the idea there was anything between us—OK? People talk. Mrs. Walker next door is the chief of the tittle-tattles and the last thing I wanted was a whip-around for a wedding as a result of poor Monica turning up on my doorstep at eight on a Saturday night with her housecoat unbuttoned. Flimsy nightie underneath, you know the kind of thing.

"'Come on in, Monica,' I said. We'd had a bit of a falling-out a few weeks previously—and then I'd been away, to see my brother in the Lake District—that's how come I missed Kilburn's latest murder this year on Saturday night. Condemned to live in flashback forever, that's Jim Graham—sorry, poor taste, Dr. Hastie.

"Monica was crying. I took her in, mopped her up, gave her a G and T, that type of thing. It did occur to me the wretched woman might have been crying over that granddaughter of hers. She got me to go down to the school a couple of years back, but for me it was too much like playing Mamas and Papas. It's a lousy school—what can you say? Kim and Dev—those are Mel's chums, tough gansta girls if you get my meaning. Monica wouldn't let them in the house and Mel took it out on her gran by running off and going to live in a squat in Harlesden with *them*.

"No, Jean, you won't find them in the same place now. The kids move on all the time, only way they can survive. You'd think the going was rough unless you'd been in a Bangkok brothel and seen the lives of the young girls kidnapped in rural areas.

"Don't get me wrong. I'm not one of those do-gooders. Just a spot hard-bitten—I've seen enough cruelty to sink SS *Globe* and life in Kilburn is a giggle in comparison with most places. Didn't stop Mel and pals from bearing a terrific grudge, naturally.

"'I'm being followed, Jim.' Monica has insisted on taking off that housecoat of hers (it's a wet night) and I go double quick to close the shutters. Not before I catch sight of Mrs. Walker staring straight in from next door. 'Hey, Monica, thinking some-one's following you is the first sign of madness,' I say, trying to laugh it off. I fetch a poncho from the hall—one of those llama numbers from the Andes—my, was that a journey to the evil heart of man: human sacrifice, the whole deal! I gave Monica a resounding slap on the sit-upon as I wrapped it round her—often quietens a woman down. Like a horse.

"No, Dr. Hastie, please don't leave yet. I'm now convinced Monica was being followed. She was in terrible danger. I'm not the kind of guy who misses out on that death-smell—pardon me—and I picked it up that night off Monica. Yes, after she began to tell me. First—you know how it is, I just tried to make the wench feel better—about herself, her house, her sad life, the whole package.

"'You look glam, dear,' I told Monica. And wrapped in that llama number I must say she didn't look bad. 'No wonder they're following you, eh?'

"Like, she went through the roof, Jean. If anyone can be described as murderous—well, it was Monica then. Makes me think poor little Mel might've inherited it. Violent streak—hate—deeply buried in Monica's case if you know what I mean, but I'm no psychologist.

"Yes yes, I'm getting there. You won't believe this, Dr. Hastie. Any more than I did.

"'You see,' Monica said when I'd apologised—and topped her up, Monica never minded a drink. 'The people who I thought were my parents—'

"'Yes, dear,' I said. I really thought she was gone, then. How many times in the past few months had Monica told me she was adopted? Come to think of it—lots of times but only in the past few months. When I realised that—after she told me—it all began to make sense. 'They adopted me from—from that woman who was a member of the Wilsford family,' Monica said and she burst into tears. 'Well, what's wrong with that?' I said. I went over to the settee and put my arm round her. Don't get me wrong, Dr. Hastie. But as luck would have it, there was just then a knock at the door—Mrs. Walker was calling out that I'd left the garage light on. I often do—they'll take the steering wheel and the seats out of a car round here if they can get away with it.

"'Don't cry, dear,' I said to Monica. 'Nothing wrong with finding you've a bit of blue blood in the old veins. Which of the Wilsfords was it?'

"'Jim, Jim!' Mrs. Walker started shouting through the door. To punish me for not replying she'll cut down the laurel hedge to an eighth of its former size and I'll be left staring at her garden shed.

"As I was thinking all this I suddenly thought 'Oh, no. Not *that* one'—but the very thought had me laughing. While Monica was crying, if you get me.

"'Not the Honourable Clemency Wilsford,' I said. 'I thought she'd been shut up on that Scottish island all those years. How'd she manage to have you?'

"Again, as I said the words a dreadful—a really laughable thought came my way. Someone was pulling poor Monica's leg. It just couldn't be—

"'Clemency Wilsford went to Germany—you know, before the War—' said Monica through her sniffles.

"'Puhlease!' I said. 'I can read the Sunday supplements as tirelessly as the next man—joke, joke.' But actually I couldn't help thinking what snobs we all are, our British race. Why couldn't Monica settle for being ordinary—like anyone else? OK, she's adopted: does that mean she has to have titled relatives, the lot? Next thing she'll say she's descended from mad King Ludwig of Bavaria.

"'Clemency was in love with Adolf Hitler,' Monica said. She was using her 'tiny' voice—there's something very old-fashioned, fifties if you like, about Monica. You'll never find that type of carry-on with Mel. Lives for now, old Mel.

"I suppose I couldn't face the implications of what Monica was saying. I mean, what do you do when a friend goes right out of it, like that?

"I thought of going and calling Mrs. Walker, who had by now huffed off back to her own house. But I decided against it. To think of the gossip—no, I couldn't do that to Monica. She has—had—a good mind, even if she couldn't do the *Times* puzzle in ten minutes—I know, I know, but some can, no names mentioned.

"'I'm Hitler's daughter,' Monica said. 'I'm being followed. Jim, for God's sake help me!'"

HITLER'S DAUGHTER

GERMANY 1937

Putzi took me to the circus today. You can walk to it across a wooden bridge over a stream, there are ducks swimming about and Putzi made me laugh when he threw bread onto the island and hit them with it. "Hurry up Clemmie," the big woman calls to me as Uncle Leader and his friends arrive and sit down in ringside seats just in front of us. "Yes, hurry up and go with your Uncle Führer," the big woman who is Magda shouts to me. A piece of paper, caught by the wind, floats over the sea which is shallow and choppy. I'm anxious—I want to go back to England—but when I see Uncle Leader smile at me I want to stay here with him. Is this the first time I have understood the Führer—does he smile at me because he secretly knows we love one another? Can I go over to him now, I ask the big woman Magda and she nods at me as the music grows louder, as the big woman settles in her chair and looks back at me and smiles, the same smile as Uncle Leader's, only more happy and it's all for me.

It grew dark and torches were lit for the circus. I was happy at last. I know I have Uncle Leader forever—and I understand the game the Führer likes to play in the garden. To celebrate the genius of the Führer we must salute, we must stand like statues, waiting for him to grant us life.

NOTEBOOK

I'm in Monica's house. It was too late by the time I left Jim Graham, to find a cab. No minicab would come: "They don't fancy coming through the Badlands to reach Bandesbury Road at this time of night," Jim said and he laughed.

I shall make no comment on Jim Graham. The transcription of his revelations and opinion of Monica Stirling this evening speaks for itself.

Now the whole episode re-runs in my head, like the video that played and replayed. Mel's face. The murder scene. And I am positive, now, that the arm holding the knife could belong to any of the girls. Everyone wants it to be Mel. Little wonder she ran off into the night.

The video ended at long last with the BBC News. Grim prognostications of success for European neo-fascist groups in the forthcoming Euro-elections. At this point Jim snapped off the TV and turned to face me. I was glad at that time that I hadn't abandoned my position by the door, despite the

37

inevitable strain that standing for long periods inflicts on my back, which was injured on disembarking from a fishing-boat on a recent visit to St Ronan's.

I resolve to record matters as they eventuate, without prejudice. I shall not think of Monica, or the house on the island, or the implications of what Jim Graham told me tonight.

But I have to speculate after hearing this extraordinary account on the possibility of Jim Graham's incipient insanity. Killing, cruelty, and pain witnessed on a global scale over more two generations have conceivably altered his perceptions. Only a melodramatic reason for Monica's distraught behaviour could occur to him.

I suspect—I know—that my old friend Monica came from the most blameless and respectable of backgrounds. The doctor and his wife in Eddleston were no doubt informed that the child they were pleased to adopt was of good English stock. The mother had not been able to afford to keep the child, neither financially nor psychologically. In the late fifties, before the Pill, these situations were commonplace.

Poor Monica—how she would have hated this tabloid rendering of her parentage. Monica liked privacy. She wanted to do good—and, as her work in the Social Services can testify, she did.

Monica's last card to me bemoaned the cuts in assistance to single mothers. "Single parents" as PC Speak has it these days.

Was Monica the offspring of England's most reviled woman, Clemency Wilsford, mistress of the man who sent millions to their deaths? Was Monica's mother a "single parent" of her day, with Adolf Hitler as the absent father?

Impossible.

Then I see the knife upraised—I see it go into the quivering bundle of grey-brown coat, Monica's hand stretched out in supplication on a pavement where blood gathers and falls into the gutter. And the knife shooting up, a triumphant spear above the tangle of limbs. The knife covered now in the same innocent woman's blood.

The girl gang did it. Wanting money for drugs. If Mel is involved she can plead manslaughter. Jennifer Devant shall represent her. . . Jennifer is the best barrister in Edinburgh.

But I'm not in Edinburgh now.

I'm in Monica's house. I shall sleep where I can. Not in Monica's room, which has been turned upside down more thoroughly than the rest.

Not in Mel's room. Old pictures of the Spice Girls and an unappetising mess of dirty black "gear," as I believe this type of clothing is known, make the prospect unenviable in the extreme. I shall clear the sofa of the old newspapers, discarded sweet wrappers, and unidentifiable items of clothing with which this house is littered.

It will be light, I calculate, in four hours.

I go round the two-up, two-down little semi—thanking my lucky stars, I admit, that the Scottish Georgian group has seen fit to grant me my pleasant flat in the New Town.

Ugliness is totally unacceptable, like chaos and confusion. Monica, in the old days, used to agree with me there. She always loved colour, and the house is saved from utter drabness by the kelims and Mediterranean powder paints she has used liberally in sitting-room and hall. Poor Monica! She certainly did let herself go: indeed, it's hard to tell how much the effect of her ruined home is due to the ransacking by the murderous gang and how much grew of its own accord.

Then I see it. I break off, and go pick it up. Before I cease speaking I record the time: 3.10 a.m. and in my hand is a brooch. I would recognise it anywhere. It lay under a battered cushion on the sagging settee. There are tiny diamonds round the frame and a central locket, containing a twist of hair. "Jean!" Monica's voice comes back to me as clearly as if we sat together now, and the voice was not a memory, echoing from that Eddleston front room with the piano, all those years ago. "Jean," the voice in my ear insists, "do you like it? It's meant for me. I found it upstairs in Mother's desk with my name written on a slip of paper by it. Shall I wear it for the end-of-term party? What do you think, Jean? What can it have to do with me?"

Oh Monica, now I look at it and turn it around, vacant smile spreading across my face like the woman in the Antiques Roadshow. For now, of course, it seems to decode itself: a dull gold locket, initials engraved on rear. Contains one lock of bright yellow hair, remarkably unfaded.

The second initial is W, worked to appear ornate and serpentine, though my throat closes in the effort to wish away the other letter, which clasps it like an eager half-moon. C and W.

"I don't know what it is, Monica," I repeat the words forty years later, this time to an empty room.

Then I see, in the nest of accumulated rubbish (a book with a broken spine, half its pages torn away; the remains of an old stuffed animal of Mel's under the cushion) an assortment of notes that spill from a purse into the threadbare loose cover, falling into its folds like paper water. I pick them up—I count them, I take them to the table and set them in a neat pile on the only available space.

At least £200 here. Why on earth didn't the ransackers take the money? So available, so easy to take and run.

Then it occurs to me: Monica's house was never entered by the assailants we saw on the video on Jim's TV. When they realised Monica was dead, they ran away. Monica was the one who caused all the damage to her own home. She was searching for something—not for money, not for this brooch. Why did Monica Stirling ransack her own house? What did she want to find?

GERMANY. JUNE 1939

"What are you doing?" Magda says. It is like a hiss, unfriendly. Then she says, "Girls who sleep with gods catch fire, and die." I don't answer. How can I? German is a hard and manly language, very precise and not like ours, full of vagaries and half the time you don't know where you are. But I can't answer Magda. I'm in a corner by myself, near the long table, with the candles in candelabras waving over all the silver and glass and food and wine bottles. Magda's hemmed me in. I don't want to talk to her. Tonight, I don't want to talk to anybody. I just look at the flames of the candles and say, "Thank you." She goes away, in the end. Good.

We drove here in a fleet of long, black cars. So thrilling.

Now there is charming piano music, waltzes by Strauss, or something, all played by the odious Putzi, a giraffe with the face of a frog, if you can imagine it, but I can't see him and won't think about him, not on this wonderful, wonderful night. Under the chandeliers, music floating round the room,

43

are the cleverest and most powerful men in the world, with Amadeus, as I call him to myself, the most clever and most powerful of all. He sweeps all the rot and corruption ahead of him like a tidal wave; he is making a new world, better and purer and cleaner.

A wonderful spectacle, the men in their medals and orders, the women in their elaborate dresses and jewels. Tonight I am in white, simple as a nun, no jewels, my pure blonde hair swept up with only a gold clip to hold it.

A little shiver runs down my long, white back, exposed by the simple gown. Is the evening growing colder, in spite of the candles and the crowd? Or am I, perhaps a little nervous, like a bride on her wedding night?

I am silent; I feel alone, somehow, in this great, important party. Suddenly, so quietly, there he is at my shoulder. "Come out with me," he says. "Walk." It is almost too great an honour. I can only nod and together we walk through the crowd, which parts for us as we go out onto the terrace. We stand away from the lighted windows, looking out on to the quiet, dark garden. So quiet—just the subdued sounds from inside the room. A little wind, carrying the scent of mown hay.

He puts his arm on mine. I feel the roughness of his jacket against my bare arm. I screw up my courage. "Tonight," I say. I can scarcely get the word out. Yet I have waited, waited so long.

44

"Yes, my little one. Yes, my darling," he says. Then the arm is gone. He is gone. I follow him, treading in his footsteps back into the room. I am dreamy, near fainting. Tonight. My wedding night, I think.

The bedroom is gloomy, with thick curtains and a lot of heavy furniture. There are dull old engravings on the walls, showing buildings and people in old-fashioned clothing. Then over the mantelpiece there's a picture of a naked woman cradling a swan in her lap. The swan is looking up at her, like a pet dog. So silly! Swans are very big and not at all cuddly. Everybody knows that. I have a beautiful nightdress, never worn before. It is satin with lace at the bosom. I have turned off the light but I cannot sleep, of course. Worse, I can hear men crossing and recrossing the hall below, loud voices, laughter and, further off, the constant ringing of a telephone bell. I can imagine the talk, the planning, the study table covered with maps and documents. Will he come? The waiting is unbearable.

Across a chair by the window lies my white dress, gleaming in the darkness. Above the fireplace that huge painting, shining a little in the gloom.

Then, louder voices, and heavy feet on the stairs and goodnights and all the rest of it. And still, I wait.

Until a gentle knock on my door, so soft that if I had been sleeping I would not have heard it. I put on the bedside lamp, and call, "Come in." He is there, just a darkened figure in the dim light of the hallway. He comes in and closes the door. He is a little tired, I can see. His eyes a little dull. There is a loud voice further off. A door slams. He drops to his knees beside the bed and takes my hands in his. "My darling. My little dove. My blonde maiden," he murmurs. The bed is high. I grasp his hands and pull him up. I rise up in the bed and put my arms about his neck. "My blonde maiden," he says. "My little darling."

He cannot insist. It is for me to act now. I unbutton his jacket and pull a shoulder free. He takes off the jacket and I pull him down, down, down onto the bed with me. I cover his face with kisses, I smooth his hair. "Are you tired?" I ask. "Never tired," he tells me. Of course not. Amadeus is steel; he is thunder; he is lightning.

Now there is a silence between us. He lies beside me on his back. He puts a hand on my breast. "Little darling, little sweetheart," he says. "Little darling, little love—sleep now." He raises up a little and kisses me, whispering endearments, over and over again. It is for me to act. "Undress," I say, "and come to bed." He gets up and moves to a corner of the room. I turn out the bedside lamp so that now I can see little but the white of his shirt.

He comes back to me, still in his shirt, and then, there I am, in that huge high bed, with my love, my conqueror, beside me.

He puts his hand on my breast and with his other hand feels his own body, between his legs. I lie very still, silent.

"Ah! Ah!" he sighs. I do not know if it is pleasure or pain. Pain? How can that be? I murmur, "My lover—my god—"

"Ah! Ah!" he sighs again.

"I have waited so long—"

"Hush. Hush," he says.

Then he is on me, his hands digging like claws into my shoulders, no gentleness now, no words. Then with one hand he grasps me hard between my legs. I try not to cry out. This is blood and fire, this is purging flame, this is a man like no other, no other in the whole world. He is breathing hard. My open eyes look into his. They are wild.

I lie quite still, feeling a surge of delight, triumph. I am his. He is mine. This night is my bridal night. He is my groom; I am his bride.

It is as if he is fighting me. His face contorts. And suddenly, it is over. He lies quietly beside me, his head on my breast. "Little darling," he murmurs. "Husband," I say quietly. His head turns, upward, his eyes meet mine. "Darling," he says "Little sweetheart. Little darling." And then, with a smile "But men must work and women must wait." He squeezes my breast and leaves the bed. I see him pick up his jacket from the floor. Then he walks away to where he left his other clothes. I hear,

"Thank you, my darling," above the sounds of his putting on his clothes and shoes. "A thousand thanks, my darling."

After he has gone I begin to tremble and feel very cold. The darkness seems thick, the air in the room heavy, as if a fog had crept in. I lie, unable to move, feeling his body on mine. I imagine our wedding, as I have so often, but the memory of his body on mine, the feeling between my legs, sometimes a sharp pain, sometimes no more than discomfort, quarrels with my visions of our union, the celebrations to follow, my appearances, on his arm, as bride and consort.

The abandoned white dress still lies gleaming on the chair. If you sleep with a god, said Magda, you burn. But I am cold, so cold.

Next day the maid comes in with coffee, and, on her heels, Bauer, secretary, confidant, and guardian of Amadeus. Salt of the earth; loyal as a dog. He apologises, clumsily, for entering my bedroom and informs me that today all the ladies of the party will be leaving. They are to return home. The men must attend to serious affairs of state. My car is waiting below, to take me to Berlin. Then, after more apologies, he stumbles out and immediately the housekeeper comes in with a jug of hot water, "for my ablutions."

These are orders. One must obey, always. I rise, wash, dress in my blue silk suit, which matches my eyes, put on my

48

blue hat, which matches my eyes, and go downstairs. I cannot see Amadeus. The door to the study is blocked by his staff. "Matters of grave importance—an emergency—no-one is to enter." This is to be expected. Men must work; women wait. The future is in his hands.

In the garden Magda is standing with another lady. Her face is the last I see before I get into the waiting car. She smiles and raises a hand in farewell.

I travel at speed through the peaceful summertime countryside, passing peasants in the fields cutting hay, a goosegirl with blonde plaits driving her flock. I am Amadeus's consort now; we have the power of life and death over the men in the fields, the little girl with her geese—over whole countries—over the whole world, that purer, cleaner world he will create.

WHO WAS MONICA STIRLING?

I'm back at the Avondale Club and glad of it.

The past twenty-four hours, since finding myself alone in the company of a brooch (badly made; late Victorian, possibly the property of old Lady Amesbury, who guarded her miscreant daughter Clemency all those long years on the island) have been possible to record only because I am here. Holland Park: not so far from Bandesbury Road, but a million miles, as I am beginning to understand, from both the suburban respectability of Monica's street and the blatant criminality of the surrounding council estates.

I am surrounded by calm, intelligent women. The confusion in Monica's house, the sense of a low-grade brain trapped in circumstances it cannot understand.

But I must refrain from judging, on grounds of intelligence. Such thoughts lead to—I must be open about this, they lead to Nazi Germany. Elimination of the mentally unfit. Eugenics. Breeding for a perfect race.

Monica stood for compassion, she helped those too poor or "disadvantaged" (how I dislike the New Britain jargon) to help themselves. What can she have thought, when she learned her parentage?

If she did, of course. And if—a big IF here—this lurid tale can possibly be true.

I set myself to find out. There are two priorities, the first being to find Mel—my wronged, misguided goddaughter Melissa Stirling. The second is to discover, once and for all: did Clemency Wilsford have a child?

But first, as I had promised myself, I cleaned Monica's little house from top to bottom. Mrs. Walker's eyes were on me as I went out again and again with black bin liners filled with the accumulated rubbish of the past months. I didn't return her curious gaze. I vacuumed, I scrubbed at the yellowing, unsavoury bath, I beat the kelims and hung them out of Monica's bedroom window to catch some of the unseasonal hot March sun which has suddenly appeared today (but no harbinger of Spring, I fear: only drought, which affects our damaged globe, even in Bandesbury Road). I showed, I hoped, that I had no intention of being disturbed while I performed these last rites for a friend who had been a proud housewife—and whose mental state had deteriorated rapidly subsequent to the death of her husband and mother.

I made my list as I worked. The sun grew stronger and flooded the semi-detached house with a bright light. A little disorienting, I confess: with the bright carpets and the foreign paints we could have been transported to Morocco. But nothing would stand in my way. When the house was clean, my first port of call was the library. In the Reference section I would find some answers. Then, whether I was welcome or not, I would call once more on the Bandesbury Road police station and ask for news of the search for Mel.

If there was no news—as I suspected—I would go to the school she had attended. The name of the school is known to me—the Isaac Newton—from Monica's past letters. Difficult to forget—as I thought somewhat grimly to myself while scouring Melissa's room—for the sad contrast between that time in history when the discoveries of Newton would lead to the great scientific changes in the world's perception of itself—and now, when science looks principally inwards: to the foetus; to the deranged brain; to the consequences of a dying world.

Enough of this. I am accustomed to long periods of work in isolation and can only conclude that sadness at the death of my childhood friend led to such introspection (for surely, disguised as cosmic anxiety, this is what it is). A night without sleep must also have contributed to an unusual—for me—lowering of the spirits, where visions of the beautiful but mournful island of St Ronan's alternated with futile attempts to recall whether Monica had ever confided anything to me about her pre-adoption life, apart from her brooch.

What did come to me was a picnic. On a shore, somewhere: but did I attend it, or did Monica only tell me about it? The latter, I think. There was a birthday cake in the story. A child's birthday then? I cannot remember—and of course Monica is no longer here to jog my memory.

In the library, I would discover if there was anyone left alive who could answer these questions. And I worked towards this goal with zest. I was proud already of the fact that I now knew there was nothing here which Monica could have been searching for. Or, more likely, she searched in vain. But I had omitted to take into account that a house where a murder has taken place recently is unlikely to be left alone for long.

By nine, the first caller had arrived: a tall, fair-haired young man. I was sure I had seen him somewhere before. He came in the front door as I pulled it open and held out his hand. "Peter Miller of Miller and Brown" was how he introduced himself.

I admit I was, and remain, deeply shocked. An estate agent—for thus his proffered card proclaimed him—when Monica is barely three days dead?

Of course. He was in the video of Monica's murder. The fair-haired estate agent standing by the house with the "For Sale" board, further down the road.

"You called the police, at the time of. . . of Mrs. Stirling's death," I said.

For a moment young Mr. Miller looked quite startled. I daresay no-one likes to be told they're on film without knowing about it. Then he smiled.

He seemed a friendly enough type; but for a reason I can't explain, I didn't trust him.

"Mrs. Stirling had instructed us to place 109 on the market, Mrs. . .?"

"Are you sure?" I snapped. I was definitely not going to correct Mr. Miller: he could call me Mrs. indefinitely. Again, I had a strong feeling of distrust—and this was further confirmed by seeing his gaze fix on poor Monica's brooch. I had just given it a Goddard's Silver Dip treatment and the setting as well as the little diamonds twinkled in a way that they hadn't since the piece went with its owner to St Ronan's—but I didn't want to think of that.

"Excuse me, Mr. Miller. I'd prefer to see Mrs. Stirling's instructions in writing," I said. The brooch was on a small table in the sitting-room (Monica had "opened up" so you could walk straight into the sitting-room from the street) and I went over to pick it up. Peter Miller looked studiously away as I did so. Surely, with an ornament of such little value, his interest must be rather exaggerated?

"The sale of 109 Bandesbury Road was a verbal arrangement," came the reply. Peter Miller looked me straight in the eye as he spoke. "I have of course brought with me our estimate of asking price and confirmation that Miller and Brown would be sole agents for the sale. All we ask, Mrs. . .?"

To avoid the candid look of Mr. Miller I scooped up a bundle of Mel's messiest clothes and started pushing them into a bin liner. Before I had time to look up, Mr. Miller made for the stairs. "We need a brief inventory, Mrs. . ." Now the voice was patronising, almost a sneer. "My colleague will come to measure later."

But of course, I thought, the house was no longer Monica's. Mr. Miller had no right to be upstairs. As I considered this, the next visitor to 109 Bandesbury Road walked straight in. In the way of estate agents, Mr. Miller had left the front door open. It was then, I think, that I realised he had a key and thus was likely to be telling the truth. Peter Miller—who had spent, I reckon, less than one minute upstairs—came down at a run, glanced at the new caller at his client's property, and stopped dead. Then, thanking me effusively for my time, he went at speed out of the house. The front door was still open and I saw him get into a smart black car (a Volvo, I think) and drive off. His mobile phone was in place, clamped between shoulder and head, as he went out of sight.

My visitor was black. He was probably about eighteen years old. He also looked in the direction of Peter Miller and for a moment we were both silent.

"I came lookin' for Mel," the young visitor said.

* * * * * *

It is almost too painful for me at this point to try and describe Chris Bradley—for this was his name—as he told me on that bright day in what I now see as the house of ill fortune that is 109 Bandesbury Road.

In my line of business—old houses and their inhabitants, revenants and inheritors—one soon develops a sixth sense. In the Borders of Scotland, as everyone knows, there is scarcely a building left standing that has not witnessed or hosted a murder, a blood duel, or simply the walling-up of an unwanted or disgraced family member.

It's in the timbers, in the shadow that falls as an innocent visitor comes through the door, to a room where a violent tragedy has played out. Or it's the quality of the light: I could swear, at Traquair House on the Tweed, that there is a darkness not entirely attributable to smallness of windows in this oldest inhabited fortified manor house in Scotland. It's more that a mist, obscuring the present, hovers in the oldest rooms. The mist of history. But this, I know, reveals a fanciful side to my nature—and it was Monica, the most prosaic character I have ever known, who would tease me about what she labelled the Celtic Twilight of Jean Hastie.

The young fellow—and still I cannot bear to describe his features or repeat his name—did, I now feel, look around apprehensively when he crossed the threshold of 109. I am very likely being fanciful again—but, after the horrific sequence to his visit to Monica's home—she the kind social worker who had in all probability looked after his interests—it is hard not to find a lurking evil wherever one may care to look. Very well, I shall try to speak of him all the same. Chris Bradley was of medium height and light skinned.

I cannot speak of him in the past tense. His promise so great, the hope and love for life in those dark brown eyes. . .

"Burnside," Chris said when, at a loss for an opening, I asked the lad where he lived. Burnside must, I imagine, be the estate where he grew up—the place where I might find my goddaughter Mel.

But then, if Mel is there, why does he come looking for her in Bandesbury Road?

Chris replied to my question without meeting my gaze: "No, Mel went—she went after—after they was all up 'ere, Sat'day. Din't she?"

"I don't know, Chris. Did she? Leave, I mean? What were they all doing? Tell me, please!"

My eager air must have put the boy off, because he hung his head and looked as if he were about to leave too, and at speed. "I thought she was here. Her mum lived here, innit?"

"Chris?" I went up to him and held out my hands—an instinctive gesture which could have back-fired. But Chris seemed to see I was sincere and he followed me into the kitchen, sparkling clean now and with a biscuit box (I had cleaned it inside as well and lined it with silver foil, to protect the still-fresh Penguin biscuits, a legacy of Monica's incurable sweet tooth).

"Have one of these, Chris. And—" I looked around in search of further friendly offerings. "Some ginger beer?" But as I said the words, a too-strong picture of Monica by the side of a loch—or on a shore by the sea somewhere in Scotland—returned to me. A picnic tea. Midges. Bottles of ginger beer with rubber stoppers that were held in place by metal rings hard to pull back: my fingers ached in remembered sympathy.

My eyes must have filled with tears, for I saw suddenly that young Chris Bradley was doing his best not to cry, too.

Very different memories, of course: he thought of Monica as old, while I thought of her as a child. Now he wanted Mel—as I did, but with more reason. They had been friends. I was bitterly aware once more that, all her short life, I had done nothing whatsoever of a godmotherly nature for Mel.

"You last saw Mel *when*, Chris? I want to help you find her."

But I knew, as the words came out, that Chris was as anxious to keep away from questions and police as any of the other kids on the estate. I was losing him, with my pragmatic enquiries and my strained, worried attitude. "Did you see her—today—or yesterday?" I nevertheless went on. Something told me I had Chris Bradley for a very short time, that he half-trusted me at least, and this was more than the Detective Inspector on the case could ever hope for.

"Yeah," came the reply. "I saw her—but I was too busy to chat an' I said I'd talk to her la'er."

"But when, Chris? Later, when?" I realised I'd fallen into the trap people of an older generation fall into when the young say they'll see you "later." It means nothing at all, just a manner of speech. "Did you know Mel came here with—with the gang and—and perhaps—without meaning to—with the knife?"

Chris's eyes went blank again. He muttered something about having to go and check something out. He left the kitchen and nothing could keep him in Monica's house a moment longer.

He did, however, say, standing on the shallow doorstep just twenty feet from where this appalling murder took place, that his sister's name was Kim and I could go and see her if I wanted to. "She wouldn't take nothin' from them," Chris Bradley said. "She said, 'I won't go in that house to rob, man, no way.' That's what she said, Mrs.—"

Chris was looking up at me as if I were his school-teacher. It was all I could do to conceal my horror at the world Mel had clearly joined. "My name is Jean," I said gently—but this, as I might have guessed, only served to frighten him off.

"Where does your sister live?" I called the fatuous question along the garden path, fringed now in this unreal sunshine with scyllas, grape hyacinths, and the odd, city-grimed primrose.

Chris turned at the gate. A tropical plant—just the kind of thing poor Monica would have detested—whipped him in the face from the next door plot. "Burnside," he said.

Then he was gone. I am able only to continue with my report of the events and findings of the day. For to describe Chris Bradley further would be counter-productive. The upset it would cause me would destroy the fragile likelihood of my finding Mel—and of discovering, finally, who Monica Stirling "really" is and why she had to die.

PETER MÜLLER

Peter Müller emailed an encrypted message to the five men of his inner circle. "I have the girl. She is half-willing. The second part of the program will soon be accomplished."

He went into the dressing room next to his bedroom, put on his dinner jacket, and frowned at his image in the glass. He did not expect congratulations from the recipients of his message. Nevertheless, soon enough they would be satisfied.

He went down the handsome curved staircase to the ground floor of the house, where a small, dark-haired man awaited him and ushered him into the dining room. There, Muller's host stood by a white marble fireplace, warming his back in front of a crackling log fire. In the centre of the room a polished table was set with three places, candles burning in silver sconces. Muller privately found this ceremonial excessive, but understood that for his host the rituals were freighted with an importance he did not properly understand.

The stocky man at the fireplace, Lord Edgar of Langsedge, came forward when Muller entered and said, "Ah, good, Muller. Punctual as ever. Alice is, of course, late."

Muller smiled. "A woman's privilege."

"So they say," Edgar replied. "Well—how's your little captive?"

"She was not entirely reluctant," Muller pointed out. "She's asleep now. The nurse is with her, naturally."

"Splendid. Reliable woman?"

"Entirely. I'm grateful you allowed me to impose on your hospitality in this way—"

"Only too delighted to be able to help," his host replied. "Take all the time you need."

"Thank you," Muller said.

"No thanks required. Anyway, we're much looking forward to our jaunt to France. A drink?"

Muller accepted a whisky, evidently from a rare source somewhere in Scotland, and watched Edgar throw another log on the fire. "Applewood," he said, "you can tell by the delicious scent." Muller nodded politely but wondered what insecurities lay behind this discreet boasting. There was some weakness there, he concluded, and knew that weaknesses were dangerous in associates. Then Lady Edgar came into the room, a woman as tall and thin as her husband was broad and tending to fat. It was as if, Muller thought, her husband had seized her substance rather like a vampire, but he knew the reality to be otherwise. The real strength in the union came from her. She greeted him. "Mr. Muller, so nice to see you again. How is the young lady?"

"Resting. It was kind of you to let me bring her here. It's simply exhaustion, the doctor has told me. Too much study, too many parties. The young don't understand their limitations."

"True," said Lady Edgar. "But they also recuperate more quickly than, alas, older people. But let her take all the time she needs."

"You're more than kind."

"Nothing is too much trouble. I think if everyone's ready we might sit down."

At the table, as a maid came and went, the three made small talk with difficulty. They had little in common. The Edgars were British people of the upper class; Muller was German by nationality but born and brought up in Argentina, the child of two Germans who had fled in 1944: a pale and weary mother who had not transplanted well and a father who lived for forty years in a frenzy of nationalism and the bitterness of defeat, until death ended his exile.

"We've just spent a fortnight at Monkstone," Lady Edgar said.

"My brother's place," her husband explained. "The Edgars have been there for centuries, since about 1740, I think it is. Lovely village, beautiful countryside, near Shrewsbury. I don't think it can have changed much in all that time, since the earlier Edgars bought the place—sugar—they had plantations in the West Indies—it's not done to talk about that sort of thing in some circles these days, I know, even if it's true."

"Unchanged," Lady Edgar said. "Such nice people around. They've been there for centuries, too. And," she added, "of course, not a black face to be seen, which is a relief."

The maid had now put down the puddings. The meal consisted of thin soup, then fish, all perhaps designed as much to avoid unhealthy foodstuffs as to please the palate. The pudding, Muller discovered, consisted of little individual dishes of crust, covering some fruit. The maid offered custard in a silver jug. Muller declined. Lord Edgar helped himself. The maid left the room.

"Pudding," he declared with satisfaction.

"He must have his puddings," his wife said indulgently.

"Of course," Muller said with a smile. He tackled his crumble diligently. "Delicious," he said.

"You should have had the custard," Edgar said. "In my opinion, a pudding's nothing without custard. But you'll be laughing at our ancient British customs."

"Never that," Muller said.

Spoon aloft, Edgar said, "Alice is right. Half the beauty of Monkstone is that it's English, same now as it's always been and, please God, always will be."

"Quite different from London," said his wife. "When I look round I can't believe what's been allowed to happen. It's a temptation to leave, but John has his duties here—"

"I'll never leave," Edgar said vigorously. "I'll stand firm, and fight back."

"Stop the rot," his wife agreed.

"The rot will be stopped," Muller assured them. "It will be eradicated."

"Did you see *The Telegraph*!" Lady Edgar exclaimed. "There are upwards of two million immigrants in this country alone. Never mind the rest of Europe. And half of them are illegals, unrecorded, living here, breeding like rabbits. We're becoming a mongrel race. The country's like a corpse being stripped bare. We need to build a wall round Europe."

"A ring of steel," Edgar said with relish.

"No-one comes in. No-one gets out."

Muller smiled and nodded his approval but added nothing. The maid had been blonde, but who knew where she came from? The manservant was from the Phillipines and who knew what scrapings from the world's gutters were working in the kitchen.

He did not want these people passing on information, one to another, in whatever shabby shared rooms in dilapidated houses they inhabited. Not when so much had been achieved and there was so much left to do.

The trio went into the drawing room for an hour and then Muller got up, apologising, saying he must look in on the girl and complete some arrangements he had yet to make.

The girl lay in a blue-green room with heavy brocade curtains at the window, muffling the sound of London traffic outside. The large bed on which she lay had a curved, gilded headboard showing nymphs and cupids at play and the counterpane was of the same heavy material as the curtains. The sheets and pillowcases were—as he had insisted—linen. He had ordered the removal of the pictures on the walls: a dog with a dead bird and a couple in early Victorian dress. His aim was to make the room as silent as possible and to remove all stimuli from the girl. She had been allowed too much pointless distraction by her fool of a grandmother. That was now over.

She lay on her back, arms above the bed coverings. Her nails were bitten and on one arm a tattooed snake ran from her wrist into to the short sleeve of the white cotton nightgown she wore.

Muller looked down at her. The tattoo could be lasered off. Her hair, heavy black with pale brown showing at the roots, could be dyed back to its proper colour, perhaps made a little lighter. Her clothes—the jeans, the cropped top, and the leather jacket—had all gone off for cleaning and purifying; he would have had them thrown out, but did not want to argue with her when she awoke. Nevertheless, she would have to wear more suitable clothes. She looked pasty, too, which, again, could be remedied.

He looked down at the figure in the big bed. Lost, like all of them, living in a morally polluted world without passion or energy, fed on junk food, addicted to alcohol and drugs, their minds taken over by the worst music, the worst films, the worst ethics—but she had good blood, this girl. She could be saved. Tomorrow, the work would begin.

Back in his room Muller put his jacket on a hanger in the dressing room and sat down at the computer to see what his core group had made of the earlier message. He was not surprised at what he found. From Vienna, George Drago (Muller could picture the square, pale face and small angry eyes) wrote, "If a man is sent to pick up two parcels and only comes back with one, you wonder: 'Will the second parcel ever materialise?'" The response from Lachaume in France was predictably more polite: "I congratulate you on having succeeded with the first part of the plan, but would be grateful for news of the progress of the second part." The responses from Grigorieff in

69

Russia and Toscano in Italy were much the same and it was left to Leyden in Holland to burst out, "The girl is one thing, Muller. The money the other. What about the money?" Muller swore under his breath. Even routed halfway round the world, even encrypted, messages could still be read, if there was a will to read them. What had persuaded Leyden to be so indiscreet? His only reply to all five men was to reiterate, in coded form, the date, time, and place of their meeting. He was certainly not going to send any further messages.

He thought the key to the problem might be that strange woman he had met in the dismal house in Bandesbury Road. He had searched it once, with no result, and when he had gone back to search more thoroughly, there she was with a vacuum cleaner, bin bags, and dusters.

At first he had taken her for a cleaner. But her blouse had been silk, with an odd-looking brooch at the neck, and her shoes, though ugly, looked expensive. She spoke fluent English, too, with a slight accent he could not identify, and she had an air of confidence, although, he thought, she had been naïve enough to accept the fact that instructions on paper from a dead woman might have some validity. Then there was the boy, Chris, from the council estate. She had so calmly let him in, apparently without fearing what one of these savages might do.

And when he left, it looked as if there was some understanding between them.

So who was she? He'd soon know. He'd photographed everything, her picture was now with supporters all round the world. Someone would know who she was. The boy was expendable; he'd need to be taken care of.

JEAN HASTIE'S NOTEBOOK

I shall never cease to regret the fact that I waited before going in search of Kim, Chris's sister.

Something about the idea of penetrating one of the estates in the Bandesbury area daunted me: I must freely confess it, though I am not one to expect absolution from anyone. On my own home ground, in the worst slums of Edinburgh, I would be able, I believe, to field the jibes and taunts with which I would inevitably be greeted.

But here—the language is unknown to me. I could see that Chris spoke to me as he would have addressed his teacher or a social worker. The Girl Gang, with Kim and perhaps a frightened, violent Mel, was not an appealing prospect. I needed a companion, or perhaps, for I am seldom anything other than honest with myself, a protector.

It did not occur to me, however, that I would find such a figure in Jim Graham. Indeed, my heart sank when, turning into the doors of the Banesden Grove Library, the nearest library in this area of deprived families and philistine suburbanites that remains open (a few hours a day at least), I saw him sitting studiously at a desk near the window.

There is always something irritating about going off on a research project and finding another person there before you. In my day at Edinburgh University, there was such an abundance of materials that a long wait for a necessary volume seldom, if ever, took place. I and twenty others might be engaged in identical voyages of discovery without the galling need to join a queue. This in Edinburgh has sadly changed over the past twenty years. Here, in Northwest London, it is hardly worth remarking that a shortage of books is inevitable. I saw, as soon as I entered, gaps on the shelves where once important works of reference and historical interest had been stored. These had been, I suspected, thrown out rather than borrowed, and a kind of kiddies' corner was all that remained of the Banesden Grove Library.

My comments on this were neither understood nor appreciated by the staff when I joined. I made my way, despite a consistently unhelpful attitude, to the stacks indicated. I had asked for Twentieth Century History. Here a long gap ran along the wooden struts and I must have let out a sigh of frustration at the total absence of the works I sought in my pursuit of Monica's identity.

"Dr. Hastie, I hope you will share my treasure trove!" Jim Graham said, beaming, tapping me on the shoulder, causing me to swing round. On his breath was the faint smell of gin—the type of gin one finds in far-flung posts of the ex-colonial empire. I remember wondering how this Foreign Correspondent of past days managed to supply himself with "Bombay Sapphire" or whatever the name of the revolting spirit may be. But I suppose anything is available in London these days: the Empire has struck back by exporting its poisons—and its peoples—to poor Britain, thus changing her identity more than anyone at the time of the dear Queen's coronation could ever have dreamed.

"Eva Braun, I presume!" Jim "guided" me to his table. I saw it was liberally piled with books on Germany, the Weimar Republic, and included—I did not say this was what I had come in search of—a study of the illnesses and impersonators of Adolf Hitler called *Doppelgangers* by Dr. Hugh Thomas. Taking up the main part of the cheap desk, however, was an unlikely copy of *Burke's Peerage*. This, I saw to my further annoyance, was open at the page of the Amesbury-Wilsford family.

Wilsford, I should now explain, is the family name; Amesbury the title. The latter descends through the male line. Only in Scotland, where justice has historically been more frequently obtained in these, and in other matters, may a title go down to the eldest child, irrespective of sex. These thoughts made me wonder whether Clemency Wilsford had possibly been the eldest in the family. Had her infatuation with Adolf Hitler grown from a misplaced power complex, a case of transference as a result of being overlooked in the stakes of inheritance? These possibilities I will file on my return to Edinburgh. There is neither time nor space here at the Avondale Club to open a full dossier on the Monica Stirling case.

I began to realise in the sad little library in the long, ugly street that is Banesden Grove, that this is what my childhood friend's death has become. A "case." Something too explosive to discuss with police, and too sensitive to bring up with the refined ladies up from the country who reside here at the Avondale Club. A daughter of the greatest villain the modern world has ever known and the scion of an aristocratic English house living here in a corner of Northwest London.

"See that?" says Jim. He has forced me to sit opposite him at the desk and the Wilsford names look at me upside down from their prolific family tree. Let me hope to God I can prove that poor Monica had nothing to do with them.

"A shooting," Jim says in the cheerful voice he appears to adopt whenever a shocking or tragic matter comes to mind. "Few weeks back, apparently."

I looked in horror at the wall by the window that he indicated. Paint had been scraped off and a section of wall had crumbled under the impact of a hail of bullets. What had once been a fine edition of Audubon's birds, donated in all probability to Banesden Grove in the days when there were still philanthropists, had been shattered by the shot-gun blast. Red and gold leather bindings were peeled away, some tatters stuck dutifully back in place with sellotape. I believe this was the first time I felt physically sick since coming south to find what had happened—and why—to Monica.

But there were more urgent matters. With an unsteady hand, I turned back the pages of *Burke's Peerage* and examined the possible antecedents of my friend.

Lord and Lady Amesbury had married in 1920. Their eldest child was in fact a son, Jack (The Honourable John Wilsford). Then came three daughters, of whom Clemency Anne was the middle one. There was no further mention of Clemency. I was not completely surprised. Regrettably, noble families are no different from the rest, when it comes to obliterating the record of family members who have brought shame to them.

The brother, Jack, had died two years previously. He had never married. The youngest sister, Laura, had also died single in South Africa a decade ago.

But here was the anomaly: the eldest sister Artemis, married to Viscount Ray of Riddlethorpe, was a widow and lived at the address of her defunct brother, Amesbury House in Wiltshire. Jack had lost all his money, perhaps, and had to sell up to his brother-in-law. Whatever transpired, there is only one living relative of Clemency Wilsford. She is Artemis, Lady Ray.

"We better head off down there, Dr. Hastie," Jim Graham said, when I looked up from the page. I frowned, an unnoticed frown I fear, as Jim expressed the identical thought that had come to me. The jovial tone had gone out of his voice and he was heaping up Hitlerabilia into a carrier bag, prior to carrying his booty over to the desk. A group of under-fives started bawling in the enlarged "Video Section" as their club ended and it was time to go home.

I found myself landed with half of Jim Graham's trawl, *Hitler: The Myth*, the Trevor-Roper (of course), and new volumes proving the responsibility of all Germans for the war years and Hitler's holocaust. The weight of information, of plots and counter-plots, of Hitler's every minor illness and final madness in the Bunker, drove me into Jim's car, grateful for a chance to off-load the books into the back seat.

I should have gone to Burnside to find Kim. If Chris had given me her name, there was a good chance she would speak to me, tell me who led the Gang to rob, and then to murder.

I could have saved Chris's life. Instead, I climbed into Jim Graham's ancient Mercedes and we set off then and there for Amesbury, the little town under the chalk downs—a town horribly spoilt, I fear, by its close proximity to that eyesore and tourist trap, Stonehenge.

ST RONAN'S 1940

The sea was calm on the night Nurse Christina McVey was called to the island and although it was ten o'clock the skies were still clear on that long, summer Scottish night. Had it been winter, and dark, with the seas rougher, her journey might have been difficult, even impossible. But a night-time summons was as commonplace to Kirstie McVey as one in the daytime, for Kirstie was a midwife and babies arrive, day or night, when they want to.

Rob, the oarsman, looked back to where she sat at the stern, her brown leather bag beside her on the wooden seat, and asked, "What would be the name of the lady requiring your services, Mistress McVey?"

"I don't know that," she told him. If she had known, she might well not have told him. Kirstie was known for her discretion. In the throes of childbirth women curse their husbands, call on the names of men who are not their husbands, may say many things even worse, secrets that will not bear the light of day.

Kirstie McVey had been a midwife for twenty years and had never once told what she heard, or guessed. But on this occasion she knew no more than Rob. The only permanent resident on the island was the housekeeper of the house overlooking the sea. Her name was Jessie Nairn, and she was a widow and past the age of childbearing.

It was still light when the boat grated on the shore of the island. Rob jumped out and pulled the boat higher up onto the sands, then held out his arm to support her as she leaped for dry land. Jessie Nairn was already waiting for them. She was a short, wide woman. She came down the beach in her old-fashioned barred shoes and print dress, a brown cardigan over her shoulders. Without greeting Kirstie, she said to the boatman, "Rob, we'll no' be needing you till the morning. You'd best get back while there's some light." Rob frowned and opened his mouth to speak. It would be a longer haul back, with the tide against him; he was tired and could have done with a cup of tea in the kitchen, waiting, in case the midwife decided the woman should be moved to the mainland. Mrs. Nairn did not allow him to say anything, just told him, "On your way, now." He nodded and moved to the boat, pushing it out again into the water. He would not argue with Jessie Nairn, the voice of the laird, who gave employment to many in the locality.

Mrs. Nairn turned and began to trudge up the beach, Kirstie following. She, too, thought it would have been wiser to have made Rob stay, at least for a little while, until it was clear they did not need him. But she followed on until they reached the house and entered the empty whitewashed hall, where Mrs. Nairn spoke to her for the first time. "She's at the back," something which hardly needed saying, for Kirstie could hear the woman groaning from halfway up the stairs.

Kirstie, still behind Mrs. Nairn's straight back, saw the housekeeper flinch a little. "She's in a wee bit of trouble," said Mrs. Nairn. She took her past several doors, then through a door to the back of the house: servants' rooms, Kirstie guessed.

Kirstie's practised eye took in the room and the woman lying on a narrow iron bedstead, and she did not like what she saw. The room itself was small and narrow with one window overlooking the hills behind the house. Apart from the bed, it contained only a painted chest of drawers and a small table. The paint was peeling on the drawers, and the small table beside the bed held only a spoon, a medicine bottle, and a Bible. The air in the room was hot with the warmth of the day, and rank with the smell of sweat and blood. The woman on the bed arched her back, threw her head to one side, and howled like an animal. The howl came to a crescendo; then died. Kirstie, kneeling at her side, saw movement at the door.

The housekeeper had taken a step backwards. Fair enough, Kirstie thought. Many had no taste for this sort of thing, would flee if they could. Kirstie wouldn't let her. "Will you stay for a moment, Mrs. Nairn? There may be one or two things you can help me with." To the woman on the bed she said, "Be brave, my dear. I'm here to help you now.

"Turn the light on," she told Mrs. Nairn. Under the harsh light from the naked bulb overhead she parted the woman's legs and, as the woman was gripped by another burst of agony, she made her diagnosis. "How long has she been like this?"

"Since this morning," said Mrs. Nairn from the doorway. "This was not meant to—the baby came early—"

"Aye," Kirstie said in an easy tone. "Babies will always be too early or too late. They've no idea of time, that's the difficulty." But she knew from the state of the woman, the bed, and the bad smell in the room that this had been going on far longer than Mrs. Nairn would admit. The woman had been in labour for a day or longer. She should have been called earlier, but she had long ago ceased to be surprised by the lengths people would go to to conceal a shameful birth. The woman's pulse was alarmingly fast. The woman moaned, she rolled her eyes, she contorted, she shrieked. "There, there. I'm here now," said Kirstie, but she did not believe that the woman heard her voice. There is a point where pain—and only pain—rules

the mind and the woman in labour had reached it, reached it some time ago.

"Will I go and boil some water?" asked the housekeeper.

"Thank you, Mrs. Nairn, but will you first open the window? It's a little stuffy in here."

"Will she not take a chill?"

Kirstie was fairly sure the window was closed in case a random group of holiday makers strayed onto the beach, as sometimes happened, and heard the woman's cries. "It's worth the risk for the sake of the fresh air," she said. "Have you given her anything to eat or drink?"

"She didn't require anything."

You offered her nothing, thought Kirstie. And Kirstie also noted Mrs. Nairn's use of the word, "required."

"Ah, well," she said noncommittally. "She might manage a drink now. Would you be good enough to open the window, set some water to boil, and then bring back a flannel, a tumbler, and some drinking water?"

Mrs. Nairn went to the window and wrenched it open, yet only pulled the sash up a few inches. Then she left the room. Kirstie calmly tugged the eiderdown from the bed, rolled it up, and put it in a corner. She did the same with the blood-streaked top sheet. She eased the sweat-drenched pillows from under the woman's head and put them with the other bedding. She

85

straightened the stained bottom sheet. The woman, she noticed, wore a nightdress of fine cotton, with embroidery at the neck Kirstie was puzzled. If she had none of her own, why was she not wearing one of Mrs. Nairn's nightdresses? It looked as if Mrs. Nairn had raided her employer's closets for this expensive garment and given it to the woman, who must be a relative, or a friend's daughter she was hiding away for the sake of the family.

The woman howled again, the great bump of the unborn child rearing up as her head thrashed to and fro on the bed and her eyes rolled back until there was little of the pupil to be seen. All for nothing, Kirstie thought: the child would not be born tonight, or tomorrow, or maybe ever at all. They might both die, that was the truth of it.

An operation, a caesarean, was the best choice. On the mainland Kirstie would have had no hesitation in calling a doctor. But here they were on an island. The message for her to come had been delivered by Elliot, the strong but slow-witted boy who lived somewhere about the house and handled the heavy work. After delivering his message he had gone to the pub. Rob had the better boat and was the better oarsman so he had brought her here. But now Rob was gone, Elliot ensconced in a pub on the mainland. Neither of them would be back until morning. If the woman did not die overnight she might well *bleed to death in the boat. Any decision she made would involve a risk to mother and child, but Kirstie knew what she must do. Kirstie would not wait for the boat. She checked the woman's racing pulse again and noted the softness of the woman's hand, like a baby's.*

Mrs. Nairn came in with a basin and a carafe of water. Kirstie sponged the woman as best she could, rinsed the cloth—soaking it with drinking water—and held it to the woman's lips. She sucked. Kirstie gave her more. Over her shoulder, she said, "Mrs. Nairn. Things are not going too well here, as I suppose you've seen. I'll need your help."

"What are you going to do?"

"She's very tired. I don't think she can do much to help herself, or the bairn."

Jessie Nairn was rigid, her face a mask. She was terrified, Kirstie thought.

"First, we'll take away the pain. Then we'll take away the baby," Kirstie responded. "Will you fetch me the kettle of boiling water and another basin?"

"I have it boiling now."

Kirstie bathed the woman's face again and spoke soothingly to her. Desperate eyes met hers, with some vestige of recognition, but the moment of consciousness was soon gone, as another wave of pain swept over her.

Kirstie opened her leather bag and was holding the forceps when Mrs. Nairn came in with the steaming kettle and another enamel bowl.

"What are you going to do?" asked Mrs. Nairn.

Kirstie took the kettle from her, poured water into the bowl, added disinfectant, and then soaked the forceps. Mrs. Nairn winced as she heard the clank.

"We'll get the baby out."

"She'll make an awful noise."

"No, she won't," said Kirstie, taking a brown bottle of ether and a packet of gauze pads from her bag.

"Will the baby die?"

"I can't tell you. But you'll have to help."

"There's no-one else," said Jessie Nairn, as if to herself.

"That's a fact," Kirstie agreed. With a steady hand, she poured ether on a gauze pad. She brought the pad close to the woman's face, keeping her own head away to avoid breathing the fumes. The woman's wide blue eyes were suddenly alert, for a moment, until they dulled, then closed. Kirstie quickly flung the pad of ether out of the window.

"Don't you go fainting on me, Mrs. Nairn," she warned.

"I'll do what I must," she muttered.

"I couldn't give her enough ether to prevent all of the pain I am about to cause, so you'll have to hold her still."

The woman moaned something that sounded to Kirstie like "Amadyss." Meanwhile Mrs. Nairn, no longer able to prevent herself from showing her fear, held on to the woman's shoulders as Jessie knelt between the woman's legs, struggling to get a hold with the forcep on the baby's head. The woman groaned and cried out in protest at the unnatural intrusion.

As soon as Kirstie had the baby's head in a grip, the woman cried out, flailing and wrenching her shoulders from Mrs. Nairn's grasp.

"You'll have to hold her legs," Kirstie said. There was no turning back now.

"What's her name?" she asked.

There was a pause. "Clemmie," Mrs. Nairn replied.

"Well, Clemmie," Kirstie announced confidently. "It'll no' be long now. So be a brave girl and keep as still as you can."

The small body, blue as blue ink, lay motionless on the bed.

"Have you any ice?"

"Ice—no."

"Get some water, cold as you can." Mrs. Nairn left the room and Kirstie cut the umbilical cord and propped pillows under the woman. She did not see attempting to revive the child as a priority. The child was probably dead and had been for some time. Only when she had done what she could for the mother did

she turn to the child. As she did so, the baby, a girl, gasped and gave a choking cry. Kirstie picked up the child and the woman on the bed said, "My baby."

"Mrs. Nairn!" she shouted down the stairs. "The water— and some sheets."

She went back to the bed. "You'll be all right now, my dear." The woman, Clemmie, tried to speak and could not. The baby lay where Kirstie had put her, on the floor, on one of the pillows. She was making a snuffling noise.

Kirstie went to the door again. "Mrs. Nairn. Where are you now?" She started down, only to find Mrs. Nairn coming up. "There'll be no clothes for the bairn?" she asked. The house-keeper shook her head.

With the sharp scissors she kept in her bag, she cut up a sheet—pure linen, she noted—and wrapped it round the baby. She put the child at the mother's shoulder.

"My God, Jessie, what have you got yourself into?" she asked.

"For good or ill, you'll leave tomorrow morning on the boat," said Jessie Nairn.

Kirstie spent the night looking after the mother and child. At dawn, she dozed in a chair beside the bed in which mother and child lay sleeping. Later she rose, made tea and toast for the mother, and brought a little broth she found in the larder.

Mrs. Nairn was nowhere to be found. Clemmie, propped up in the bed, apologised: "Thank you. I'm sorry if I made a fuss."

"It was very hard for you. The bairn seems well, after all that. What do you think of calling her?"

"Isolde," the mother said.

"A lovely name," said Kirstie.

Mrs. Nairn emerged at the front door with an envelope in her hand. "Your fee," she said, holding it out.

"Thank you, Mrs. Nairn. I require no fee for this night's work," Kirstie said.

In the boat, watching Rob's back as he bent over the oars, Kirstie could only wonder: "Isolde. What sort of a heathen name was that?"

JEAN HASTIE'S DAIRY

Notes On Visit To Amesbury House

Tea served in the library. Strawberry Hill Gothick. The unfortunate addition of Art Deco chairs and table. "Clouds" Morris carpet in excellent condition. No sign, as is so often the case in this type of establishment, of messy or indulged pets.

Lady Ray is elegant and well dressed. Tea: scones and anchovy paste. The ceilings have been repaired: good workmanship in evidence.

My National Trust connections turned out to be more than enough in the way of a calling card. I go so far as to flatter myself that the name Dr. Hastie was not unknown to Lady Ray. Almost immediately, our hostess invited us to walk down the Long Hall, pointing out various portraits or Ray ancestors (state of preservation: good) by Van Dyck and Sir Joshua Reynolds. She was quick to remark how much she regretted not selling St Ronan's House to the Trust. Expressions of remorse were slightly overdone—Lady Ray still has a pretty face and the air of a great actress. There was a trifle too much fluttering of her chiffon scarf; and heavy sighs at the mention of the Dutch financier who had acquired and then abandoned St Ronan's. Perhaps Lady Ray suffered from the ennui of advanced age and a long winter in the English countryside and would answer our questions without any very great effort on our part.

I did not, alas, have an opportunity to test this impression. My companion had already boasted on the drive down the M3 to Amesbury of his past relations with Her Ladyship. At first, I paid no attention. I was at the wheel, having indicated to my companion that the aroma of a gin of far-flung provenance would prove undesirable to the constabulary of Hampshire and Wilts.

He lit an odious small cigar as he spoke, clenching it between his teeth as if in emulation of a screen character from America, a country I have visited but once. Americans care only for money, a subject to which I have seldom given more than a moment's thought.

"Older women. . . Yes, Artemis was a great lay," mused this impossible traveller. "She was on the stage, y'know, Jean. Not the real stage—more like a theatre for naked women. In those days they could stand there bare-arsed but if they moved," here he had the temerity to put his hand over mine on the wheel, "if they moved just one little bit, then the curtain was brought down and the audience was plunged into darkness. It used to be great sport to see if we could get Arty Miss Carter—her stage name—to run off the stage in a fit of giggles."

The best way to silence a bore is to maintain absolute silence. I was so intent on doing this that I found myself shooting past the Palladian gates of Amesbury House. I had no option but to go right on, almost to Stonehenge. My state of mind was not improved by this mistake, nor by the loud laughter from my companion at my oversight.

I record this interlude—plus my unfortunate reversal onto the pineapple gate stoppe, which are now rare and found only at Syon Lodge, to remind myself, when I compile my file later, of the extreme provocation I was under on the occasion of accepting an invitation to take tea at Amesbury House.

This provocation contributed to a certain brusqueness in my manner when addressing Lady Ray. My companion was, I knew, leering at our hostess. I witnessed Lady Ray consumed by an emotion I could not identify, after hearing his muttered compliments. The chiffon scarf went repeatedly up to cover the mouth. She appeared to be shaking. She voiced further expressions of remorse over "losing" the island near Mull.

"Lady Ray, may I enquire whether your sister"—here the old lady bristled and all at once looked her true age—"whether

Miss Clemency Wilsford had—at any point before going to live at St Ronan's—"

"I say old girl," warned my unspeakable companion, "watch it, eh?"

Lady Ray, I observed, now looked at me with what appeared to be deadly hatred. "Whether she gave birth to a child," I finished. "There is a reason—a good one—for my enquiry. I give you my word as a Trustee of the Ancient and Historic Buildings of Scotland."

Lady Ray now employed the silent treatment, unnerving me considerably. I could hear my stomach rumbling as a result of the too-rapid ingestion of scones and anchovy paste.

"Certainly not!" Lady Ray said eventually.

It has been observed that persons of superior intelligence know, above all, when to deploy their advantages. Timing is everything. I dug into my bag, retrieving the brooch from Monica's house. Its modest diamonds were eclipsed by the Amesbury House chandeliers. I put it down on the table, causing the tea cups to tremble (Rose de Sevres, no chipping nor stains: rare these days, but proof in my opinion of Lady Ray's artificial nature, of a love for the flowery and unreal).

Lady Ray stared at the brooch. I turned it over so she could see the initials. I exhibited the preternatural calm of a hostage negotiator.

Lady Ray let out a long sigh.

I would not at this point have looked away from my hostess, down through the open library door to the Long Hall and the stone-paved vestibule beyond, if Lady Ray had not herself suddenly glanced—with an expression of great alarm—in that very same direction.

A figure in a nurse's uniform was crossing the tesselated marble floor, carrying a metal tray. I could not see what was on the tray. There was a strong likelihood that medication of some kind was being taken upstairs. The figure paused momentarily at the foot of a particularly handsome Jacobean staircase— oak and well maintained—before ascending without a further glance at Lady Ray or her guests.

Lord Ray, I know, has been dead some years. Does she have a secret guest, someone desperately ill, perhaps?

It was Jim Graham who now seized the moment. Lady Ray no longer concealed her paroxysms of mirth. Her mouth trembled violently with barely stifled laughter.

"Artemis!" Jim Graham scolded. "We have a serious matter to discuss here. If your sister did in fact give birth to a child—a daughter—who was then given up for adoption. . ."

"No!" she cried.

"Then I must inform you that this daughter now has a granddaughter and that this granddaughter is in very great danger. You must prepare yourself for a shock: your niece was brutally murdered last week. You cannot have known this, of course. . ."

Lady Ray leaned forward across the tea cups and the circular occasional table, edged in gilt. We could have been an Edwardian painting entitled "The Secret." Though ill at ease, I must admit I was impressed by Jim Graham's handling of this delicate matter.

"Her name was Monica," said Jim Graham.

"Isolde," said Lady Ray.

The next minutes were chaotic. I recall the brooch tumbling to the floor and the lock of youthful yellow hair falling from it. Lady Ray swore in German. I suddenly remembered that, according to the story, it was Lady Ray who had been sent to rescue Clemency from her romance with Adolf Hitler, shortly after the outbreak of war.

Indeed, she had been involved, along with other members of the family, in stratagems to "unite" the two countries long after hostilities had been officially declared. Pictures of Blackshirts in London's East End and Hitler smiling in a sunny garden with a Wilsford sister on each arm, returned to me.

"It all went so horribly wrong," Lady Ray said. She made no pretence to hide her amusement now, and Jim Graham stared at her in open revulsion, measuring this woman against his possibly invented memory of the naked "actress" who had been such a "great lay."

"We all adored Hittles," Lady Ray said. "He had such charm. He would have taken this country from the mean little men and restored it to greatness."

"Lady Ray," I said, "I have had the need to study my friend's bank accounts in order to try to penetrate the mystery of her death. Are you aware that your niece was receiving a great deal of money on a regular basis? Would you be so kind as to confirm for us the origins of this stipend?"

Though this was a total bluff, my instinct was correct and the timing of my question was perfect. Lady Ray stared at me in horror. I concentrated on evaluating a fine chinoiserie chest, late eighteenth century, upon which cavorted gold dragons and other imaginary monsters.

Before us was a true monster. I felt strongly that my goddaughter Melissa Stirling had become a pawn of destiny. She was the only direct descendant of Adolf Hitler. Had she been abducted by unscrupulous admirers of the evil man's doctrine?

"Monica certainly did start to throw it around at the end," said Jim. "It was very unlike Monica to buy a drink, for instance. But she was happy to do so, at the end. She paid; she paid! Irish coffees all around, for instance."

"Lady Ray?" I said patiently. Jim and his Irish coffees were nearly bringing the whole thing down. "The stipend?"

"Go and see Maitre Paul." The very old woman rose from her chair. Her whole frame shook. I thought for a moment of a frail tree, a birch perhaps, bending in the face of a gale.

Then the nurse reappeared, descending the staircase, walking with a squeaky-shoed formality through the Long Hall and into the library where she stood beside Lady Ray with quiet authority.

I should have realised it before: Lady Ray was a seriously ill woman. The medication was for her. She had escaped from the upper room against orders from a doctor and was using our conversation as a pretext to momentarily evade the implicit orders of this silent attendant.

Lady Ray took a malacca cane from the side of the pear-wood Récamier chaise longue by the side of the tea table and leaned on it heavily as she left the library. The nurse took her employer's arm, guiding her down the length of the Hall and up the staircase to the upper floors of Amesbury House, leaving us alone without another word.

INTO THE HEART

It was eight in the evening when I arrived at the Burnside council estate on a hunt for Kim.

Leaving the Underground Station at Banesbury Grove, I entered a different world indeed from Amesbury House. Jim Graham did not join me.

Here in the "estate"—which has so little to do with the country estates purchased with City bonuses and kept up by trust funds administered from Guernsey—the aura of fear and sadness is palpable, in very stark contrast to the manicured meadows and mossy woods of Lady Ray's demesne.

Burnside is a brisk ten-minute walk from Banesbury Grove, and not a pleasant one. The towers of a misconceived utopia from thirty years back loomed out of the dirty air and light rain. I stopped by the entrance to a collection of redbrick buildings, tall and forlornly covered in graffiti. It was already dark. Lights were either broken or unprotected by glass and ready for the next vandals to attack.

There is no room for poetic expression regarding what happened next. Just the bare facts.

A man has been killed. A man lies dead on the asphalt, under a sodium lamp which shows blood spilled on rough ground and the faint flesh tones of an outstretched palm. His eyes, wide under the ugly glare of the lamp, stare up unseeing.

The man is Chris Bradley, and he lies dead and alone in the main forecourt of Burnside.

Who named such a place "Burnside"? I suddenly saw a real burn, in my native land. Trout in a brown pool. Nasturtiums in summer, a joyous yellow and orange in the dim colours of the Scottish hills.

The shallow brown pools are Chris's eyes as he looks up so trustingly at me. The bright colour comes from the lamp, with its deadening effect.

They wanted him dead. They killed him after he came to see me at Monica's house.

But, be calm, Jean Hastie, I told myself. Who knew about his visit?

Now I hear the wail. The girl runs from Burnside House, the first house on the estate (now my eyes are becoming acclimatised to the dark) but she stops when she sees me. I clamber from my kneeling position, to say:

"You're Kim, aren't you? Oh Kim I am so—"

102

A shot rings out.

I, Jean Hastie, have never been a courageous person. I fear and detest violence, any form of aggression, any reminder of war. I have not even attended Edinburgh's military parade: the sight of the muskets and bayonets, the Ghurkas and Highlanders, fills me with a strong antipathy to man and his martial instincts.

But this evening I stood my ground.

A silence as complete as that which had greeted me on my first arrival at the estate followed the gunshot. Kim disappeared into the first house, with its ramp and gloomy walls, slashed and obscenely larded with impenetrable words, a testimony to poverty and a final lack of hope.

The silence went on. Why, I found myself thinking, does one shot always seem to demand another? The movies perhaps: the quick, casual delivery of death which satisfies audiences with its staccato repetition.

In that silence—fanciful though this may sound—I heard the first heartbeat of an ineradicably changed and changing England. (England, yes, but not the country north of the Border, where justice may, if we claim autonomy, be served.)

I heard the birth cry of a people who had hoped against hope for justice, and, in its refusal, had turned first to anarchy and then to something infinitely dark, evil, and persistent,

103

something which had lain dormant for all these many years and which had now returned to haunt and inhabit the land.

I could have sworn that when I looked away from Chris and up again to the orange blaze of the lamp, I saw a figure there. Diaphanous, scarlet-haired, as ugly and ferocious as a demon's mask at a children's Halloween festival. Then she was gone. Someone from within the barricaded flats had rung the police at last and the sirens sounded along Banesbury Grove before turning into the maze of one-way streets with which the Council presumably tried to discourage quick getaways.

I waited for the police, feeling like a ludicrous target in the white mac I'd taken down to Lady Ray's "just in case," and with my shoulder bag (like Monica's, I thought with pain) swinging against my side.

Then the alarm was screaming. The blue lights flashed.

I agreed to accompany the police to Banesbury Grove Police Station.

Here, I was given tea, and an apology for the absence of anywhere to sit.

Would I mind standing over at the desk and telling them why I had been at Burnside and what I knew of Chris Bradley?

But of course I could only tell them I knew almost nothing at all.

MEL

The Avondale Club is bustling today. The Women's University Challenge Tournament is to take place, televised, in our main Hall. Unsuitably to my mind, a male compère will preside.

I have declined to take part. Events of the past two days have been chilling, gruesome—I cannot help but take some of the responsibility for the death of Chris Bradley. And I feel a chain of evil happenings, as yet unknown and unpredicted, are about to unfold.

"This is most decidedly not like you, Jean."

The woman who sits opposite me at the table by the window overlooking the tennis courts and camellia bushes is Jennifer Devant, Edinburgh QC and a friend of thirty years' standing.

At any other time, I would have been delighted to see Jennifer. But her quick mind and shrewd ability to derive insight from the slightest hesitation or inflection of the voice are not welcome at present. I must ponder the fact that Monica's

105

hysterical visit to Jim Graham the night before she died was caused by truth rather than a sick mind's fantasy.

She was indeed the daughter of Adolf Hitler and Clemency Wilsford. I gaze over the grapefruit segments and tea and coffee pots on our breakfast table. What could that have possibly been like for her?

And Mel. To what fate has she now succumbed? At the police station, I kept everything I knew about Chris Bradley to myself. Why? Because Mel is my goddaughter perhaps. I cannot help reflecting that all this is becoming absurdly Mafia-like and unreal.

But the unreal does happen; and nowhere more often than in this city of a thousand tongues and a million identities; this crossroads of crime and subterfuge; of inequality and lies.

I remember Lady Ray's last words to us, her sudden air of capitulation as she suggests that we "find Maitre Paul." When Jennifer, spreading Old Oxford marmalade onto her toast, looks across at me, I recognise the gaze. Jennifer knows something, as she would put it, is "up."

I begin to talk, to tell Jennifer Devant of the improbable— the absurd!—discovery I have made about my friend Monica Stirling since coming south after her death. I tell her about the ransacked house; the incredible revelations of Jim Graham; the visit to Lady Ray. I unleash a tale wilder than any madwoman's.

Duly, Jennifer's eyebrows rise, her slight smile fades away. But I do not stop until I am finished.

It's hard to describe my wounded feelings when it becomes clear that Jennifer Devant, QC doesn't believe a word I've said. When I reach the killing of Chris Bradley, I stop dead. Jennifer waves me to go on. Downstairs, an audience applauds at the Cambridge graduates. I recognise the voice of Mary Worsley, the Newnham don who makes mincemeat of her opponents on talk shows. A quotation in Greek from *The Iliad* comes floating up the stairs to us.

"Go on, Jean," Jennifer says quietly.

So I describe the walk from Banesbury Grove Underground Station down Banesbury Road after leaving the police station.

I knew somehow I had to go back to Monica's house, after what happened at Burnside. Some clue would come to me there.

It was about ten at night by then and I didn't like the knowledge that this was the route poor Monica had taken, with her shopping in one hand and her shoulder bag across her shoulder and strapped across her stomach. But I told myself I owed it to her to go back to 109.

It was the least I could do. I had never been there for Mel or Monica when they needed me most. I would be there for them now.

The car coming along Banesbury Road seemed to be coming straight at me. I had the sudden instinct that it would leave the road and mount the pavement when it reached the right angle to run me down.

I jumped. There was no alternative. I crashed through a low, neatly trimmed hedge and brought down a rickety bird table. A window opened; a light came on.

The driver and his passenger accelerated and drove on.

But I saw them.

Here I was glad for the presence of Jennifer Devant at the Avondale Club. For it was almost too nerve-wracking to recapture what I saw one more time.

"Peter Miller—that's the estate agent I told you about—was at the wheel. Beside him—well, she had long blonde hair—it could have been a wig, but if so a very expensive one—a fur coat, white—a lot of make-up—you know, what they call drop-dead gorgeous, Jennifer—"

"From your state of agitation, my dear Jean, I believe you saw Mel in the car," said Jennifer Devant.

"Yes, yes," I said, grateful to the point of tears for the speed of my friend's thought processes.

I had fallen into the yard of Mrs. Walker, the neighbourhood Watchwoman.

"I went on to Monica's house," I said, "and I found the place had been ransacked, all over again."

All my neatly-packed bin liners had been torn open, their contents all over the place. Mrs. Walker's astonishment at the scene had not been welcome, either.

"Mr. Miller and your goddaughter Melissa were looking for the same thing that Monica searched for in vain," said Jennifer, even quieter than before. A waitress came up to clear away our Continental breakfast.

"What?" I said.

"On your first arrival at Monica's house, a fairly large sum of money was left untouched. You concluded that Monica herself was responsible for the mess."

"Yes," I said, uncertain now in the face of Jennifer's sharp, professional manner.

"If Mel is being held captive, then the people who have her must be the searchers. You must find what they were looking for."

"BUT WHERE?" I said. My voice came out louder than I'd intended and the gaffe was greeted by laughter from one of the contestants in the hushed and tense Main Hall.

"Maitre Paul, of course," Jennifer said briskly. She rose, showing she had a full day ahead.

"But—but where is he?" I stammered.

109

Jennifer Devant slipped on the jacket of her neat Harris Tweed suit and started to pick up briefcase and handbag.

"Maitre Paul, originally German, was the lawyer for most of Hitler's top brass. A visitor, along with Bormann and Speer, to the Bunker in the last days of the Third Reich. A close friend of Magla Goebbels. She must be quite old by now."

"Who?"

"Leni Paul," said Jennifer Devant. "I can find her for you. She lives in Paris."

A LETTER FROM MONICA

Dear Jean,

It is late—I have lost your number. Oh Jean, for God's sake come down from Scotland and help me. I am in danger—and so, Jean, is the globe—the world—the planet—you will think me mad, Jean, but was I ever like this with you? Please believe me—

I am on board the Dover to Calais ferry. The letter, with its envelope postmarked Mar 2nd, the day after Monica was killed (she must have walked on that Saturday all the way to Banesbury Grove post office), is secured against the gales by my haversack, which is slung across the front of my body and is holding the frail paper in place on my knees.

From time to time I pick up the sheet of cheap paper, already yellowing. It has journeyed from Edinburgh to the Avondale Club to my lap. The words dance before my eyes. Malodorous newspaper cuttings are held together by a

111

half-broken paper-clip and are poking from the top of the office envelope. A window of see-through material, intended for the recipient's name and address, shows snippets from the press: "No-go zones in East Germany," reads one; "British neo-Nazi Party in . . ." reads another.

Behind them, a bundle of similar reports: fires in immigrant hostels; clubs "liberated" from "foreigners"; ex-prison inmates, convicted for racial incitement, addressing the cream of Germany's military. Denmark, Italy, Le Pen's France: Monica's collection grows in length and prominence as the dates become more recent. Since she learned who she was. Poor Monica. She did the devil's homework, all right. And for her pains she was killed.

JEAN HASTIE'S DIARY

I am not one to indulge when it comes to travel. The idea of luxury seating, obsequious attendants, and all the rest, makes me uneasy: I would frankly prefer to donate this money to the poor of the country I am about to visit. The children who cannot find enough to eat in the slums of Naples, for instance. The wretched, exploited AIDS sufferers in Africa. As for those who dress up in costume, taking the Orient Express to Paris and Venice: why, it is quite repellent to contemplate. The beaded dresses from the thirties, the pearls, the false elegance—

I think of Clemency Wilsford. A foolish, upper-class girl, in love with the vilest man ever to walk the earth. . .

I must explain, Jean. I tried to tell Jim Graham down the road, but he is too sure he knows everything and he looked at me as if he thought I'd gone crazy—

The letter shakes in my hand as I read. An attendant passes—tall, young, dark hair held in a pony-tail under his cap, eager to please in this climate of jobs as quickly gone as they are found. I push the letter under the knapsack again. I am not a rich, expensive-looking traveller, and he walks on, descending the stairs to the First Class Club Lounge. I struggle to lift Monica's letter, my fingers blue with cold, to read it again. I consider running down to the First Class Club to let them all know: their world is in terrible danger. Whether they believe themselves liberal, or faintly conservative, or even admirers of our Iron Lady, the royal blue Queen who still rules so many hearts, the world they know is about to be irremediably and horribly swept away.

I think Jim does believe me now, Jean—but it is unlikely he can take any steps to prevent the disaster which is on its way. Jean, when you read this you must go to the Prime Minister— you must alert the Foreign Office—only you, with your credentials as a historian, can gain the ear so urgently needed now—

It seems incredible that this tremulous, concerned being, alive and agonising over the future of the human race on paper, should now be dead in real life.

They want Mel. They need her, Jean. It is too vile and wicked to describe.

Mel, my daughter, the great-granddaughter of Adolf Hitler. She printed out those terrible photographs, from her computer, of the dead Goebbels child in the Bunker. They gave her drugs, and she went with them.

I entrust Mel to you. You are her goddaughter. Save her from evil.

While we were playing hopscotch in the playground at Edleston School, they were waiting and planning. Do you know, Jean, just how many Nazis there are in this smug little island of ours? Only in the past few months, since the death of the good doctor and his wife, have I begun to learn.

And so it went on, page after page of cheap, lined paper. I tried to imagine her desperate attempt to find peace, donning the "negligée" which made Jim Graham sneer. Her panic, as she faced another evening as the secret daughter of the world's most evil man, her fear for her own granddaughter. Was Mel naturally bad? How much nurture, and how much nature, was there in the violent, aggressive child?

Finally came her unsteady run down the road to Jim's house; the curtain twitching as Mrs. Walker watches her go by; her return to 109. The shambolic house empty of provisions; the donning of skirt, jumper, and overcoat. Then out to the Banesbury Grove post office, bag strapped across her stomach. Still quite early. A March afternoon shading into evening.

The gang coming down the street.

The shouts.

The pale hand raising the knife.

Monica falling; blood spouting onto the pavement. . .

"Madame?" A voice from behind made me jump. "Excuse me, Madame, it is the fire drill. You will please go down the ladder to the lower deck."

The tall attendant who had passed me before looked intently at me as he spoke. Then he moved on, looking back a few times to ensure I obeyed instructions.

It was only as I descended the ladder that I realised a bell was ringing loudly.

The little car ferry universe, with its rude, shouting lorry drivers and angry businessmen, was held up by the bell. A sailor threw us all life belts. No-one put one on.

Then the clanging stopped. There was only the rough slap of the sea and the pull of hawser and chain. One of the French drivers yelled an insult about Algerians to another, and then both of them, cigarettes dangling from their lips, laughed and spat.

I did nothing to remonstrate them. I knew myself a coward. I thought of Monica. She would be ashamed of me. In her mind I stood for good, even if she had found herself to be marked by evil.

I went into the lounge where the humbler ticket holders were permitted to take shelter from the elements. It was nearly empty: just one man in a dark raincoat sat by the spray-lashed plate-glass window.

I returned to the letter.

They want the number, Jean. I turned the house upside down for the number. It has gone. But—I almost remember—that game we played in the playground—how did those numbers go?

That was all. Monica signed off with that tall, neat M I remembered so well.

A short time later, she was dead.

NOTEBOOK

The Rue Danube on Paris's Left Bank is the unexpected head-quarters of Maitre Paul.

The area is more affluent than in the sixties when I studied at the Sorbonne. There are boutiques and art galleries where once there had been shabby cafés and little shops selling candles and soap. Tourists have clearly taken over the Deux Magots and the Flore, where pseudo-philosophers such as Jean-Paul Sartre and Simone de Beauvoir used to air their pretentious views.

I crossed the Boulevard St Germain and set off in search of Rue Jacob. The street was restored and smartened, fit for a prominent lawyer's office, rather than the garret life of Jean-Luc Godard (another bête noire).

I prepared myself for what I might discover. Jennifer Devant, after scribbling the name and number on a legal pad, warned me of Maitre Paul's almost supernatural quickness of mind, and of her extreme rudeness should she perceive herself to be in the presence of a "dolt."

I needed to know the facts surrounding Monica's parentage. I must be shown birth certificates and proof of Clemency Wilsford's actual relationship with Hitler (if any such relationship could exist: Jennifer's caustic comments on the Führer's testicular condition were both crude and specific).

Most of all, as my barrister friend insisted, I must discover what financial arrangements Hitler made for his child. "The will, Jean," said Jennifer Devant, QC. "If there was an arrangement for Monica, the sum must be gigantic by now! Nazi gold!" And my incorrigible friend had rolled her eyes and lit a cheroot, always a sign of pleasure on her part.

My intentions, on meeting Maitre Paul, must be clear: I would not be deflected from the answers I so badly needed, however unusual the speed of this octogenarian's mind.

I had to know how and where I could find Mel. The car that had nearly run me down in Banesbury Road was as long gone as the infamous Fiat Uno allegedly responsible for the death of Princess Diana, just a stone's throw away from here. There would be no hope of finding Mel unless Maitre Paul co-operated with me.

The building in the Rue Danube was at first impossible to locate. Private *hotels particuliers*, dingy from the outside but boasting fine courtyards and showing glimpses of Aubusson tapestries and discreetly lit oil paintings, served as reminders of the hidden life in France. What if Maitre Paul's address had simply vanished? What if the ancient lawyer was in fact dead? Questioning any surviving relatives would be tricky: I saw, in my mind's eye, first scorn, then disbelief, and then anger, at my requests for information on the private life of Adolf Hitler.

Yet, there is something of the dogged, the Scottish, in my character. It was worth the while of Maitre Paul to collaborate (an undesirable word: I banished it as soon as it came) with me in the matter of Mel. Unlike my friend the hard-nosed barrister, I was not out for retribution at all costs.

None of this, as it transpired, was of the slightest use to me when it came to finding Maitre Paul. After finally entering the foyer of a shabby building which had HOTEL DANUBE in faded letters above the door, rising in an ancient lift at the side of one of those twisting staircases in which Paris seems to specialise, and walking to a door of thick oak with the words MAITRE PAUL in gold lettering on a plaque beside it, I was annoyed to find that there was no-one there to answer my ring.

The boy at the reception desk had yawned when I asked him for the lawyer. A chambermaid, in a full black-and-white outfit with frilly apron, waved a feather duster in the direction of the Maitre's suite with much the same combination of silence (my least favourite characteristic of the French, I own, a maddening *je m'en foutisme*).

121

This was a hotel with surprising touches of comfort. As my eyes became acclimatised to the gloom I noted that a splendid pair of *fauteuils*, almost certainly genuine Louis XVI, stood along the passageway; and an oval portrait of a wistful girl, definitely by Greuze, hung on the wall near the Maitre's formidable and impressive oak door. Were these from her collection? For a moment, thoughts of Hitler's looted treasures filled my mind, and a sense of repugnance at the expropriation of Europe's finest works of art made it difficult for me to concentrate on the interview ahead. Were there lost masterpieces waiting behind the door by the Impressionists, by Cézanne, Monet, and Van Gogh?

A very slight sound behind the door roused me to the importance of my errand here in Paris. There was the smell of urine.

The noise behind the door—first a rubbing, sliding sound and then a series of muffled bumps—stopped abruptly. Then the lights all went out.

Now I began to feel alarmed. Even the head of the balustrade was unlit and the lift door totally invisible in the blackness. There was nothing else to do. I pushed my knee against the heavy oak and threw my body against it at the same time. The door swung open with ease. I was in Maitre Paul's apartment—her "chambers," her bureau, her private art gallery.

I have heard it said that contact with a stranger when half-asleep in the dark is the most disturbing experience it is possible to have. At first, there is familiarity. Then the organism rouses itself to fight. What has been unthinkingly fondled must be kicked or stabbed: disposed of straight away.

This was my experience, except for the added complication of a fragrance so strong that the creeping smell of urine was quite vanquished. What was this fragrance? *Muguets, bleuets de champs*? I only knew it to be overpowering and expensive. At first, I found it welcoming. As if the luxurious ambience provided by the scent (later, I was to discover, Guerlain's *Après l'Ondée*, a blend of wild iris root and gentian) meant I had done no more than step on a rug, a fur maybe, or an ineffably soft needlework carpet.

My hand reached for a light switch. A chandelier blazed suddenly overhead, in the rose-muralled, over-scented passage of the lawyer's private rooms. A cat—a Russian blue, with unpleasantly slanting eyes—strolled from the end of the corridor.

An ancient, painted, sequin-jacketed woman lay dead at my feet. In her hands: a long piece of paper. Even as I stood there, standing quite literally on top of her, I could read the words: "To Peter Miller from Maitre Paul."

JEAN HASTIE'S DIARY

I write this in the train. A group of English schoolgirls giggle as a long-haired, dark young man passes them in the corridor and refuses to return their cheeky glances. A priest, opposite me, is deeply engaged in fondling some kind of electronic object. Does it give him comfort? Do Catholics lavish their care on imaginary beings such as a Tamagotchi more readily than Protestants?

She was small. Maitre Paul was as shrunken and simian as an exhibit in a museum of past wonders: a dwarf at a Sicilian court, perhaps. Her suit was Chanel, circa 1968. In such an outfit the *bonnes bourgeoises* of Paris and its outlying suburbs cried out in dismay at the "Revolution" brought about by the students. I saw their little gilt chains rattling on TV as they spoke against the preposterous notions of freedom, equality, and individual libertarianism which those foolish months fostered.

Maitre Paul's suit had once been raspberry tweed. Now the fruit has turned a darker hue from blood spilled down over the

125

elaborate frogging with which Mme Coco Chanel distinguished her otherwise unremarkable suits.

Blood, from such a bloodless corpse. To steal from the Scottish play: who would have thought the old woman had so much blood in her?

But of course I am in shock. Trauma. Yes, I am traumatised. The word is as bland and meaningless as all the other politically correct phrases we are fed by the social services these days.

My quandary: I should find the police, and I should go to them in London.

Then the words of Jennifer Devant come back to me: "Never apologise, never explain. Not that you ever do, of course. Hard to tell what beats in that breast of yours."

Why do I think of her now, as the TGV heads like a great reptile through the banlieus of the world's most corrupt, most civilised city? Am I urging her to make me abandon the train, my mission, everything?

For it is a mission by now. I know I should return to London and tell the police. I should tell them why Monica died: because a gang of children were sent to find something in her possession, and, panicking at her resistance, killed her.

I should tell them the gang was paid in drugs. That Chris Bradley died because he wanted to tell me the truth.

Peter Miller. Peter Müller. He presented himself to me as an estate agent. But who is he really?

I left his letter in Maitre Paul's hands, but not before I read what was inside. Replacing it was the hard part: the tiny fingers brittle as twigs, snapping as I forced the paper back into the tiny palm.

I should be on a train back to London.

Instead I am on a train to the South of France.

I called Jennifer Devant before I left, but there wasn't time to tell her much.

My mission remains the same: to find Mel and make her safe.

Come with me, Mel. All this is a ridiculous mistake. Come and live with me in Edinburgh and I will teach you to trust again, even to love. . .

How dull and flat France is! Mile after mile of factory chimneys, of grass as winter-grey as the withered cheeks of Maitre Paul!

Jennifer Devant again: "You left Monica's house the last time quite certain that she ransacked it herself, searching for something. Why did you say you thought it might be a number? Your number, Jean? The number of someone who could help her? The number of the police? Try and think, Jean. . ."

The priest nudges my knee as he leans forward to pocket his beloved toy deep in the folds of his robe. Two schoolgirls decide to come into the compartment and take their seats. The dark, long-haired young man comes along the corridor again and the reason for their entrance is clear: they giggle again at him. Sure enough, the young man pauses. They go scarlet. He frowns. He gives me a quick glance and walks on.

The book was on the sofa, under the arty Indian cushions Monica liked to scatter about. It was by the brooch, but I was too busily excited by that to think anything of a battered book, a primer of skipping games and chants and hopscotch, played by young people all over the world.

"I think," I said to Jennifer Devant, "that I saw a book with number games with a page torn out."

"Didn't you and Monica play those games together?" Jennifer asked. This time she forgot to light a cheroot, and looked dreamily out of the window into Holland Park Avenue, as if expecting to see a whole army of children jumping over the pavement flagstones as they made their way to school. Jennifer could make you remember anything—but that is why, no doubt, she is considered the best barrister we have in the North.

Mel is in the South, near a village whose name I have carefully memorised. She is with Peter Müller.

I shall find Mel and bring her home.

As the train gathers speed, the last words of Monica's letter haunt me with the rhythm of the playground games we used to wait for so impatiently, through interminable lessons—and sometimes through punishments with a strap of hard leather.

The numbers. How did they go?

NOTEBOOK

Given Maitre Paul's spidery announcement, at the foot of the missive to Peter Müller, that she was determined to give to another "what I will not give you," I knew I had to act, and to act quickly.

I did not believe I could escape either arrest from the police or murder at the hands of Muller and his men. I knew my only option was to run. A French prison would have me locked away for the murder of Maitre Paul until their nefarious plans were carried out.

According to the letter, she would do as he requested, or she would die. She would leave "the information" under her door, with a tip of the paper spilling out on the landing.

There was now little time to lose. April 20, the birth date of the Führer, was originally proposed by Maitre Paul herself as the appointed day for the "meltdown." If she continued to betray the cause, then she would answer for it immediately.

Muller believed Maitre Paul held the secret of the numbers. Also, Monica. They were both now dead.

But one thing became rapidly clear in Maitre Paul's letter: Maitre Paul had undergone a change of heart. She loathed the Nazis: now she looked back on her life and bitterly regretted her association with them.

She loathed the "Duke and Duchess"—here I wasted a precious five seconds wondering whether the Windsors, with their famous affiliation to the Fascist movements in Germany and Italy, were the royal couple to whom Maitre Paul now turned her contempt. She wished never to hear the name of Adolf Hitler again. And, most vehemently, she would ensure the inheritance the Führer bequeathed to his only child would go to causes set in the world for the promulgation of good, rather than evil; this inheritance, tens of millions in gold, held in a Swiss bank.

Peter Müller must not expect to be admitted by Maitre Paul, to her apartment in the Rue Danube. She would have nothing to do with him in future; nor with his protégée, the offspring of Hitler's daughter.

Then came Maitre Paul's shaky signature.

Though there was no mention of Monica in Maitre Paul's letter, there was much about Mel, seen as a new threat, spearhead of a movement which will thrive on her inheritance. Late in life, though the confidante of Speer, Goebbels, and Hitler himself in his last mad days of illness and collapse, Maitre Paul had not wished to die branded with their names or their cause.

Had she told Jennifer Devant all this while I travelled across the Channel, assuming my visit would come as a surprise?

Again it was impossible to tell. But here I was, straightening the tiny, crumpled body, hearing the sirens on the road below.

And here came the maid. La Bonne, in her frilly apron and shiny, cheap black stockings and skirt. She stopped when she reached my side, at the entrance to the flat, and she stared down at the dead body of Maitre Paul.

I am not accustomed to hitting people. I picked up my knapsack from the floor and brought it down on her head.

THE USES OF SCENT

I undressed the charming young bonne and I donned her frilly cap. Pushing my own clothes into my haversack with some difficulty, I put on her skirt and her black sateen blouse.

My guide books to France had served as excellent weapons. I had stolen them quite brazenly from the Avondale Club library (two volumes of the meanderings of Augustus Hare in the early years of the century). I pushed the heavy haversack into a rubbish bag and stepped over the bodies of Maitre Paul and the servant in order to make my way from the narrow hall onto the landing of the Hotel Danube.

I knew where I had to go. The heading on Peter Müller's abusive return note to the lawyer had given me the department in Southern France.

I counted on Augustus Hare to do the rest, for there was certainly no time to buy modern guides and maps, with both the police and the Muller gang on my tail. I would have to count on the unchanging character of rural France: somehow, while disregarding instructions to "take a chaise" or "enjoy for one franc the excellent fare at this auberge or that."

I must get to the village, maybe the fortified chateau, where Mel is, I am convinced, incarcerated, and waiting for the final day.

I haven't had time to reflect on the "European Disunion" to which Muller briefly alluded in his blackmailing missive to Maitre Paul. I wonder if there might not be some connection with the coming elections to the European Parliament?

The date given in the letter, while being obviously familiar by reason of its being the birth date of Adolf Hitler, also rings another obscure bell with me.

At that point I could not ponder this, any more than I could dwell on fugitive memories somehow connected with the mysterious numbers to which Monica piteously referred in her last cry of help to me.

It is a race against time. I forced myself to go at a steady pace down the corkscrew staircase of the hotel, mop and bin bag in one hand, dustpan and brush tucked under my arm in readiness for a necessary stooping pose in the foyer, should the *gendarmerie* of the *7ème arrondissement* rush in as I descended.

I thanked my Maker for the calm and presence of mind with which I have been blessed since birth (though intelligence, prudence, and an excellent education have also been constituents of my "unflappable" nature).

An old woman sat at the desk of the Hotel Danube. She stared vacantly at me before returning to the magazine open on her knee. I looked to right and left and then froze in my tracks.

On my right, here came the *gendarmerie*. Police sirens sounded in the nearest main thoroughfare to the Rue Danube. The hotel was clearly their destination: they charged along the Rue Danube as if there were no other habitations in the miserable thoroughfare at all.

On my left, where the unimportant road crosses another within a hundred yards of the hotel entrance, a group of men in business attire walked purposefully along, led by Peter Müller.

He made no effort whatsoever to conceal his identity. His fair hair, which appeared to have grown more luxuriant since the glimpse I caught of him in the fast car in Banesbury Road, brushed the collar of an English tweed overcoat of an expensive cut. A brown trilby sat at an angle on his head.

What was I to do?

I dislike to draw any parallel between the workings of the intellect of a superior member of the human race such as myself (a woman in her prime, highly qualified) and a man engaged in the business of indulging in sexual relations.

However, I have read that, in order to postpone ejaculation, such a man learns to distract himself: to count, to conjugate verbs, or whatever he prefers. Forcing myself to walk at an unconcerned pace down the narrow street was much like that process.

If I hurried, either the police or Muller and his colleagues would have me dead before I had reached the crossroads no more than fifty metres distant.

My first thoughts, in this effort at distraction, concentrated on the significance of uniform in the history of warfare, oppression, and occupation.

Life consists of an alternation between reflection and action: surely there is no better example than the innkeeper's wife's story in Diderot's *Jacques le Fataliste*.

At this point, to my annoyance, I see that there is only one shop on the corner. I walk with casual indifference towards it. Behind me, the police storm into the Hotel. In front of the Hotel, the group assigned to relieve me of the "numbers" which will in turn release an unimaginable sum of money from the vaults of a Swiss bank, slow their pace and watch the police. They act like innocent bystanders, expensively dressed gentlemen of assorted nationalities out for a stroll, unpleasantly surprised by a raid on the neighbourhood hostelry.

Above the nineteenth-century facade of the shop on the corner, there is the word *Parfumerie* in Belle Epoche gilt. I had hoped for vegetable stands, or at the very least a *patisserie*: quickly overturning shelves bearing such goods can cause enough mayhem to aid an escape, preferably into a waiting *camion* on the pavement of the intersecting street.

NOTEBOOK

I was not so fortunate. Surely when the Germans marched into Paris, the effect of their tunic-clad uniforms must have inspired awe, instigating the necessity for surrender, which would not have been caused by a motley crowd—some poorly clothed, others in fine garments—all demanding the right to take over the city?

DIARY

I walk into the *Parfumerie*. I feel the eyes of Muller and his "Europeans" on me.

I was fully aware, as I went along the street and into the delightful old-fashioned shop gleaming with glass phials of every conceivable fragrance, of the reason that no-one had attacked me yet.

I was in uniform—the uniform of a chambermaid—and the fact I walked sedately down the street, perhaps on an assignation, more probably to buy cleaning materials so badly needed for the much-neglected water closet at the Hotel Danube, caused neither comment nor alarm from Muller or the *gendarmerie*. To demonstrate more forcefully my role as a menial, I carried a large black rubbish bag. However, I made a mistake.

A chambermaid may walk about in the street, but she is not expected to go into an exclusive *parfumerie* in the heart of Paris's *Rive Gauche*. She must content herself with the purchase of cheap perfumes, from the Galeries Lafayette or some such department store. She may carry a rubbish bag—or, as it is inelegantly termed in Britain, a bin liner—but she certainly must not take this bag into an establishment which boasts that it has served discriminating tastes for more than a century.

Muller and his men followed me in.

DIARY

The lady standing behind the counter stares straight at me as I approach. I first feel her incredulity: how did this middle-aged chambermaid have the effrontery to enter her shop? Then I feel her anger: she summons her voice to enquire in a steely tone if I have mistaken the address. She indicates a humble haberdasher's visible halfway down the street. Her arm shoots out as she speaks.

I am reminded of the Nazi salute. I stumble, my hand sweeping across the counter.

The bottles break. The samples, with their grotesquely large spray attachments and fraying rubber, suggest ancient afternoons of passion ignited and then quenched in clouds of "Joy" and "*Sous le Vent*" and "Jicky"—names dancing up at me from the glass containers.

The shop proprietor comes out from the back room. A short, stocky man, he sees the police as they run into the Hotel Danube.

I fall to my knees. One last large chartreuse bottle smashes on the tiles.

Muller and his men stop behind me. I hear them fidget and cough.

The proprietor runs past my prone form to the door, pushing past them to catch the *gendarmes*.

The fragrance—so strong that it overwhelms even the assistant still paralysed behind the counter—sweeps across the airless space that is the *Parfumerie*, provoking a sense of renewal, of winter followed by the first shoots of spring. Wild iris roots, the smell of Monet's garden, flowers young and rain-drenched that hold within them the seeds of their own decay. The scent is *Après l'Ondée*, the scent that dominates Maitre Paul's claustrophobic apartment in the Hotel Danube. Her murderers hold back, fearing a trick, an arrest, unconsciously reminded of their most recent evil deed.

And while they stand there, I crawl along the far side of the mahogany late Empire *vitrine* and into the back room.

I shed my uniform and extract my haversack from the black rubbish bag.

Next: an eminently respectable Scottish lady walks briskly down the street behind the *Parfumerie* and enters a haberdashery shop.

Both police and Muller's men race past me, as I deliberate between one type of thread and another. My hands, I am happy to note, are steady enough to experiment with threading a needle. For good luck, I purchase a charming little thimble, probably late eighteenth century, from the collection of the Marquise de Crécy. In any case, it is enamel, with a motif of forget-me-nots around the base.

CLEMENCY

They said I looked like a baby. So innocent. Hitler loved the look of youth around him. I was a flaxen-haired Brunhilde with a swastika brooch pinned to my bosom. . . and they were all so kind to me, though it took days to appease him at Berchtesgaden after the English were so rude about us. . .

We were to be married. He embraced me at the altar. After I left, he sent flowers. . .

Now I have a role to play once more. It reminds me of the time he and I made lists from Tatler *of the lords who would join the Nazi Party. . . many more these days, of course, and by no means all lords, all walks of life, as my father would have put it, with his little laugh under his white moustache. So many people who want to save our country, save Europe from the rot that threatens on every side.*

I apply the foundation first. . . thick, white. If I am no longer flaxen-haired, then my flaming mane will return our people to the vision of Nordic goddesses as surely as if I were young again. And my eyes, so porcelain blue, my skin so pure and white—and a mouth as red as desire: that's how the Führer put it when we met and kissed on the day I went out in my fighting uniform on the Hesselberg. Where are my gauntlets now? I would never wear gloves to swear allegiance to the party: gloves are for luncheons. Always carry a spare pair of white gloves on the bus and change as you approach the Duchess's house.

Hitler would have loved Edward to be King. I went to the gallery, Dadda was a peer after all. I listened to the Abdication speech. So sad, so tragically, unnecessarily sad to lose a King who could have worked with Hitler and brought happiness and unity to us all.

The worst of it was that the foolish man in charge of foreign press relations—Putzi Hanfstaengl was his name—took out his handkerchief and wiped off all my beautiful make-up.

Keep in line with the blonde womanhood the Führer expects, Putzi said. He dabbed at my porcelain blue eyes, ringed with pencil and mascara. I hated that man, and I believe he hated women, and so did Heinrich Himmler who burst into my hotel room in the dark and tried to assault me. They wanted to destroy the lovely Englishwoman who brought secrets to Hitler and would one day be his bride.

But now I have a mission to perform. I left the coast of England behind, and set out for Europe which will be mine someday. My sister waits anxiously in her house which is like a tower in a fairy tale.

After Peter telephoned, she helped me go, my faithful sister, and I came over the sea to the land I am now destined once more to bring to sanity, to save.

"The car will be waiting for you at the port," my sister said. "And here is the medicine Peter sent to strengthen you in your task."

And they all stared at me with admiration: I Clemency, who have been hidden away more than half a century, stepping out in my furs ready for the new age.

I found her at the Hotel in Paris, when the car stopped at the end of the street.

My dear Leni, what a charming apartment you have. . . of course, when you heard my voice you had to let me in.

Don't change your mind Leni, I said. You are needed now as much as I am. We knew the wish of the Führer, that we would continue with his work after he was gone.

I have come for the numbers, Leni. You can't refuse them to me. We used to eat and drink together, you and I, we were photographed together at the Osteria and at the Games. You small and practical-looking: Oh Leni you were never a beauty as I was, but the Führer trusted you and you drew up his will.

151

His chief bequest was to our daughter. She vanished. My mother would have preferred her to die. But she did not, and so my mother took the baby, living evidence of all they wanted to forget. She had her adopted.

They murdered her, searching for the numbers. It was her fault. She should have co-operated with them. I can only repeat my allegiance to my party: I care for no-one, nothing else. The daughter I brought into the world loved all the scum and riff-raff. . . How Herr Hitler would have hated her.

Herr Hitler. That's how I addressed him. Always. He called me Lady Clemency. He would have had our daughter destroyed, or better still, sent to an Arbeitslager.

But Melissa, her granddaughter. Yes, Leni, I see you have her photograph in your apartment in so many poses. Melissa is our hope. They are training her to stand by the Leader as I did, to front our new pan-European movement.

Melissa, my great-granddaughter, as white-skinned and flaxen-haired as I once was. . .

"Take her back with you," Leni pleads. I still see her face, so much older and more wrinkled than my own, as she stares up at me from the over-heated hall of her apartment in the Hotel. Her eyes are rheumy. The flat stinks of scent. Leni, I was not sorry to admit the callers when they came.

"Take the girl back to England." Those were your last words, Leni.

You had lost your wits, you had betrayed the memory of the Führer. You deserved to die.

JEAN HASTIE'S DIARY

The TGV from Paris to Marseilles takes four hours, forty-four minutes. The priest left the train at Lyons and the tall, long-haired dark young man has come to take his place.

The giggling schoolgirls, pale with waiting for something exciting to happen, stand in the space at the end of the carriage where a smart Parisian has parked her Burmese and Siamese cats, and the Louis Vuitton luggage is piled too high. Each flick of a cat's tail as we enter a tunnel or slide through a cutting threatens to bring the whole edifice down.

I am exhausted from long hours spent, half-dozing, waking in terror, in the brasserie close to the station. I know the constriction in my stomach means danger: danger of a mental breakdown rather than physical fear, though it could presage both.

I am being pursued, hunted, followed. I know I am thought to carry the numbers which will gain access to the fortune that would have been Monica's and now must be Mel's. And I know myself a godmother who comes into the scene to act as God: I

155

decree that this fortune shall not be seized and that Mel shall escape the taint of Nazi gold.

The meek shall inherit the earth. I wonder, as the train slows in a landscape tinged with the fiery orange and apricots of the South, whether the priest's presence opposite me for so many miles has influenced my way of thinking.

But I dismiss this thought: the lurching sensation has returned and this time the Train Grande Vitesse cannot be held to blame, for we are almost motionless now.

I look out of the window. A donkey stands in a field. Olives make a fuzzy line along a lane green with gorse and yellow with their blooms. In the distance, hills painted by Cézanne, obeying his geometrical rules. Blue, purple: the russet orange again, cubes and planes intersecting sternly under a pale azure sky.

The long-haired man's eyes are on me, and for a second I look straight into eyes I've seen somewhere before. Eyes that turn to one side and pretend to take in the landscape of Provence beyond the window.

But then he returns to staring at me. And my heart suddenly executes a perfect somersault in my breast: these are eyes I saw on the ferry on the way here: eyes closed against the brisk northerly winds; eyes lowered in mock humility as my notes blew overboard and fluttered down the steps to the First Class lounge.

I force myself to look again. The mocking, hooded eyes are closed now, as if the effort of gazing out at so much beauty is exhausting. It comes to me, with another sickening lurch, that there is something both odd and familiar about this rubber-faced, effeminate young man. On the boat. . . the ferry. . . he was the steward. . . and then I see the hands.

And then I see the girls. They walk, bunched together, between the sleeping passengers, between the miniature bottles of wine on tables, between the hanging coats, padded, tweedy, obstructive. . .

The girls. They come like trained animals. The man's eyes are closed, but he has lifted a finger of one hand to summon them.

I rise, as unostentatiously as possible. The silence and immobility of the train lend an eerie quality to the scene. The gang of girls giggle no longer. Their deathly white faces betray their dependence on the one opposite me, deep in his feigned trance. Before Mel's army can reach me, I am down the other end of the carriage. The automatic glass door opens for me with a sweet, greased swishing sound, then closes like the gates of the Underworld.

I am inside. A toilet, a basin. . .and, yes! An emergency chain. I tug at it. Who would pull it when the train is stationary? Will the guard come? I hear the shattering high-pitched electronic scream. Then, slowly, the doorknob begins to turn.

The knife was in the sleeve, above the ancient wrist, imprinted with the brown flowers of death. Its blade was as long and thin as an adder's tongue, sharp with venom. It makes straight for my neck, whistles past my ear.

I seize the hand: the mask drops, the face riddled and pitted with years. Evil glares out at me.

I understand. The strength of the old woman is unexpected. The girls crowd behind her and push me down.

I crawl, I force my way like a dog through a forest of bare, knobbly knees. I am between carriages when I see a door open: my emergency alarm has brought panic to the train.

There is a poppy field. How red it is, red as the hair of the creature trying to kill me. . . red as the sleep the evil men sell to the children in return for their unthinking violence.

I jump. I fall. I roll. There are sharp pebbles under the poppies in a field untended and bare in patches. A thin horse stands some way off and turns to stare at me.

I am in a wood. Olive trees mostly, but also scrub left to grow high and then not cut back. The same bright gorse blooms like beacons in a dusty Provencal field.

I run into the scrub—the maquis. It tears at my clothes as I go.

The train starts again as silently and smoothly as it had stopped. Why has no-one from the train followed me?

I am pleasantly impressed by the clientèle attracted to the *Trois Frères*, the first humble auberge I came across in my country walk after leaving the TGV.

It was the headmistress at St Agnes's in Edinburgh who advised me that the surest path to success in life is to forget the failures. If being attacked in an insalubrious w.c. on a train by an octogenarian British female Nazi disguised as a man can be counted as a failure, that is: it was certainly a failure of perception on my part, for it should have been obvious that she was observing me from the moment I set foot on the train.

So I have taken my usual course in times of uncertainty: step by step, as Miss Cuthbertson used to say. One thing at a time.

First, I have neither money nor a change of clothing. I left my haversack behind in the scramble for the open door, where it now doubtlessly lies in the hands of my attacker. They have my Augustus Hare. My best Fraser tartan skirt and Pringle cashmere sweater from Peebles are also lost to me, as is my wallet with its sterling content. £500 is all I would permit myself for this particular trip. I do not use credit cards, as they are an invitation to debt and theft. I have no intention of utilising foreign currency, as its fluctuations are too undependable. I shall not handle the euro, and have written to the new Scottish Prime Minister to inform him that I am strongly advising the National Trust to refuse the euro at the gates of famous houses and art galleries. Surely we, of all bodies, may be permitted to pay as we have always done, with the pound? The reply from the English office to my request was nothing short of offensive.

The walk up from the poppy field was a harsh disappointment to a student of the Impressionists (though I have always had a strong preference for the works of Courbet). Both sides of the dusty track were guarded by tall wire fences and by Alsatians which barked ferociously as I went past them. Names of properties, *la Bastide* this and *Closerie* that, gave no indication of the type of building hidden by forbidding umbrella pine forests and by further walls and barricades. I had the undesirable sensation of being in occupied territory; though occupied by whom or what it would be impossible to say.

So the little village about two kilometres up the hill came as a distinct relief. Very quaint; almost a picture book. No dwelling under eighty years old; a charcuterie, boulangerie, boucherie, and all the rest; even a central plane tree and a game of boules in progress.

I could have wept with relief, but obviously I did not. I paused by the side of the paved area outside the *Trois Frères*, evaluated the handful of people enjoying a pastis or Cinzano at tables there in the warm spring sunshine, and then marched purposefully in.

Despite having tumbled down a railway cutting, disregarding the flinty stones and bruised olives, my Harris Tweed remained as robust as ever. I have also often noted the effect of my personality, and can usually rely upon it with some regularity in the case of an emergency. I had no difficulty persuading the management to allot me the best room in the establishment, and persuading them that my luggage was lost and would arrive in the morning. I was soon settled in, and then led downstairs to enjoy a fine *Tripes à la mode de Caen* (no nonsense about vegetarianism here in France) along with an excellent half bottle of Bandol, an unpretentious but delicious Provencal wine.

Then I called Jennifer Devant, whom I called for the second time after completing this much-needed repast. I learned that she has left the Avondale Club, and is not to be found in Edinburgh either. The news came as something of a blow, I must confess. However, for those who remain calm, as I invariably do, there always comes a solution to the most intractable of problems.

I signed the bill, adding a small but perfectly calculated gratuity, and then I went out into the village and its environs for a short walk.

Surely, if I visited the local chateau, I would find a way to alert the right person of my situation and summon both funds and help.

But who exactly is this right person?

I am in pursuit of a juvenile killer, as the police of many countries must regard poor Mel, and I have no desire to tip off the authorities until Mel is safely in my own keeping and has told me her version of events.

I suspect I myself am also a target for further attack. In the eyes of Muller and his friends I am in possession of the secret code which will release the Nazi millions intended for the wretched Monica.

Altogether, I am unable to decide whether I am the hunter or the hunted. If it were not for the pleasant sense of anonymity here at the *Trois Frères*, I would be on the verge of anxiety. If it weren't for the charming good manners of the other diners, I would sense trouble and persecution on all sides.

Here, I had nothing to fear. The young couples, the middle-aged and elderly alike, are well dressed, well bred, and a pleasure to dine among. They appear to be multi-national. I counted a Danish grandmother and her family; an industrialist

162

from northern Italy who spoke of his estates near Salerno; three Belgians; and a party of Norwegian landowners—not to mention the numerous French tables, each with its individual rolled napkin and horn ring. As my friend Jennifer Devant would say—and there is no denying Jennifer can be a wee bit of a snob—the class of the clientèle must reflect on the good table at the *Trois Frères*. She would surely have been able to point out an Austrian Archduchess or two; indeed, on passing the table nearest the door on my way out, I was unsurprised to overhear a lively conversation in German, but with that unmistakable upper-class Austrian accent, regarding the superiority of the *Boudin* served over the Saddle of *Lièvre,* stewed in its own blood with red wine.

But for me this is no light-hearted account by a *bon viveur* of a journey through France. No "horror movie," as my colleagues at Edinburgh and Aberdeen are prone to describe the classics of the past such as *Dracula* or *Frankenstein,* could do justice to the very real horror with which I was soon to be visited.

After smiling carefully at the concierge of the *Trois Frères* (I did not receive so wide a smile in return as I had hoped; there was even a quiet request for information as to the whereabouts of my *bagages*, to which I could only give the stern rejoinder that the airport authorities at Nice and Marseilles were concentrating on little else) I walked out and set off with purpose towards the crest of the hill.

I was immediately surprised by the amount of traffic in this little village.

There were not just cars parked in serried rows down both sides of the place to the *Grimaudière* (clearly a rival establishment) at the foot of the hill, but also a host of motorbikes, and even coaches—which, as I have so frequently complained to the Scottish National Trust, can instantly remove the ancient romance of a castle or fortified dwelling. Nothing distresses me more than a walled garden where the coaches are invariably instructed to moor, like metal whales in pellucid waters.

A very different class of people from those in the dining-room of the *Trois Frères* had now arrived in the village.

They were thugs, to be absolutely frank. Music blared from tinny contraptions clamped to the sides of their heads. Tattoos were visible on their bare arms. And, is if to underline the lack of suitability of their attire, a light rain began to fall.

Were these the unemployed? I was even more astounded to see this crowd of undesirables pour into, of all *venues*, the very hostelry from which I had just emerged.

I feared for my haversack and the contents of my wallet, I confess—until I remembered that I no longer possessed them. I castigated myself for believing the lie I had only just recently used against the concierge: thus are criminals caught out just when they least expect it.

I determined to press on, nevertheless. France is a country of a revolutionary nature, after all. These distinctly lower-class people, workers from a local factory perhaps, had come to protest their pay and conditions. Unlike the British, who would never be seen storming the dining-room of the Savoy Hotel in their anger at homelessness or low reward for labour, the French clearly had no qualms as far as broaching the *Petit Trianon* that was the charmingly rustic restaurant of the *Trois Frères*.

I thanked my lucky stars that I was no longer inside and caught up in the inevitable brouhaha. There was certainly not time, in my quest for Monica's daughter, to become involved in Trade Unionism and so on. I increased my pace to a brisk trot; and, possibly due to the effects of the *soufflé Grand Marnier* (supplement twenty francs but of course not yet paid for), I finally arrived fairly breathless on the crest of the hill.

There was something reassuring about finding a small school perched there. There was nothing else in the way of buildings as far as the eye could see. The rest of the village was hidden under the hill. The sound of children's voices floated out of the window into a rudimentary playground, a strip of cement surrounded by wire fencing.

Straight ahead, I saw a range of mountains so large and magnificent they could only be the Luberon. A fine, sweet air seemed to waft over from the distant range. . . and once more I was reminded of the auld alliance between the country of my origin and France. The love the Scots and French hold for each other; their joint hatred of the Sassenach; the tragic queen whose homes I used to show—how completely enthralled the French were by the melancholy romance of Mary, Queen of Scots.

I felt for a moment that the French might save me. But this was madness. The *bons bourgeois* who sat over their gigot in the *Trois Frères* would want nothing to do with a penniless Scotswoman other than to report me to the police. The *ouvriers*, to judge by the specimens recently disembarked from the coaches in the village square, would think nothing of beating me up and leaving me for dead.

A pristine rainbow formed at the base of the Luberon mountains; and—yes, I confess I was carried back once more to my childhood, oblivious to danger. The sound of an ice-cream van as it climbed the last steep gradient of the hill gave me a strange sensation of hope.

I felt close to my journey's end. That is the only way I have of describing my sudden happiness and lifting of spirits. There might even be gold at the end of this rainbow—but I didn't want

166

it, and I wouldn't take an ounce of it, not with its provenance in death, torture, and theft.

I walked along the road a while, looking down on a great plateau alive with scrub and heather and small bees which danced in the just-opening blooms.

Just below the plateau, where it dipped at last into a descending staircase of terraces, meadows, and meticulously planted vines, stood an ancient tower. It was an ancient chateau in fact: the tower, circa 1170, and the long, calm grey castle which flanked it, had been added at least two centuries later.

A cloud of white pigeons rose into the sky from the tower. A few needle-thin apertures served as windows. It was then, foolish though it may appear, that I felt my greatest hope. This hope would soon be dashed, destroyed, and stubbed out, like the finest spray from a rocket, exploded in a dark cupboard and never seen again.

But at that moment I was euphoric. The voices of school-children were perhaps responsible for my joy.

I paused before going down once more into the village.

I was, I confess, deliberating on the best method, while bereft of luggage, of washing my smalls.

I had settled on a plan for a brief wash and rinse-through of my undergarments in the *en suite* bathroom of my room at the *Trois Frères*, and I had decided that drying them on the

167

radiator in my room might—if French habits with *chauffage* were more liberal than they had been in my freezing student days in Pairs—be efficacious, when the words came straight from the playground at me.

I was once more transported to Edleston.

"Ell, Dell, Dominel. . ."

The correspondences between the old French scores and the children's games of southern Scotland returned to me. Had I not gone to the trouble, as an adult, of tracing those old playground games? I had even gone so far as to write to Monica, for we had loved the words so: "Zeenty, teenty, figery, fell."

My voice rose with the others. Of course, the words were not all the same, but, as the children raced back and forth in their Starting Games and as they fell into the chant of "French and English"—or "German and English" as it was known a century after the Napoleonic wars—we entered, without the bairns being of course aware of it—into rhythms and syllables that went back to Celtic times.

Now the children formed teams, four to a side. They paid no attention to me whatsoever, as they took prisoners, declared themselves victors, shrieked in defeat.

"Jean, can you remember those games we used to play?"

I looked even further back into the past, the shore of an island . . . the ruined chapel. . . the hopping, skipping game we played on the uneven cobbles, cobbles as old as the first traces of Christianity to reach those Hebridean isles.

"An, tan, ternera. . ." The old counting words came back to me as I stumbled down the hill, past the refined bungalows that made up the sparse outskirts of the village.

I had the code. I knew, somehow, that it was this that Monica had searched for, the words to the games. . . the chants that went with skipping and jumping. . .

At the back of the ruined chapel on the island of St Ronan's stands a man.

I am there. I do not want to think about this man. He has come to visit Monica.

She is six years old and this is her birthday. I am her best friend, I have been brought to meet her real mother and father, though she doesn't even know who they are.

Of course. The cake, with the number six in pink icing dribbled by the expert hand of Mrs. Douglas. . . the skipping, counting games Monica and I played together on the long slabs that marked the tombs of buried crofters. The number two, tan in the old sheep-counting rhyme, the symbol of diversity, the principle of strife and evil. "Three times two makes six" in Monica's high, delighted voice, as we run and hop and skip up to the cake.

And the man, a tall, fair stranger, who stands in the shadows of the ruined chapel. . . I hear him speak, and see the fair woman gaze up at him submissively. He says the numbers will bring a fortune to the child. "Isolde," the fair woman says and smiles, and she lifts a hand that wears a ring as pale blue as her eyes.

* * * * * *

I stop where the road widens, where the place with its tired plane tree and smart new red roof of the *Trois Frères* lie placidly below me.

The two small bars in the village are bursting with newcomers.

The restaurant is full, though my table, now with its napkin tidily tucked in a ring, awaits me as I come in.

I indicate that I will not be long upstairs. The French, as I had reason to know on the occasion of my séjour as a student with the parsimonious Mme de Bérenger near the Madeleine, will refuse to serve dinner if one turns up even ten minutes late. And I was anxious to sample the potage du cresson and the filet de sole Bercy promised for the evening meal.

I take ten minutes to bathe myself: I was still wet through from the showers on my expedition to the schoolhouse.

The concierge smiled with his old sincerity and vigor when I assured him that I would be taking my place very shortly in the dining-room.

"But yes, Madame." A gold tooth glinted at the back of a mouth blackened by a half-century of strong, local wine. "Madame's husband awaits her upstairs. Madame will be delighted to be reunited. . . and with the *bagages*. . ."

Before I could make any movement of my own, I was being transported to the second floor of the *Auberge Trois Frères*.

JIM'S STORY

The sight which greeted my eyes when I turned the key was a man reclining on my bed drinking a whisky and soda (with no coaster) on my bedside cabinet and smoking a pipe, which was resting in an ashtray into which I had placed my hairpins.

I do not in principle have anything against men being admitted to the rooms of female students. Like many others, I have read of the results of repression on great minds, such as Sylvia Plath.

However, the ease and familiarity of the pose adopted by the ex-journalist and Foreign Correspondent Jim Graham was such that I found my breath taken away. I shall pass over the equal familiarity of his greeting—indeed, it was little wonder the desk staff had considered us man and wife—and report the news, which is grave.

It was impossible to prevent myself from noticing that my uninvited visitor had removed his shoes, and that an unpleasant odour emanated from feet in cheap nylon socks. It occurred to me that this man was in need of a wife, without doubt: an instinct, doubtless, inbred in my generation of women reared on Doris Day films and mothers grateful for the end of war and lack of men.

The feeling was of course stifled as soon as it arose.

"A good thing you managed to ring Jennifer Devant from the bar. Better still, that an old newshound thought to ring the Avondale Club for news of your whereabouts and then was able to call in a favour and get a fast plane ride." He paused, then murmured, "Just like the old days."

And how I wished he had not. But Jim continued seamlessly:

"You know, Jean, it's always been a dream of mine to have an apartment in the South of France. What do you say to a flat-hunt, when all this trouble is over? Something in Juan-les-Pins—a little place with a balcony, what they call a glimpse of the sea. Whaddya say?"

Jim Graham's information, after he had, at my insistence, extinguished his pipe, was as follows:

"I have to tell you," Graham proceeded, "that you are in grave danger. Only by assuming an identity as your spouse was I able to enter this auberge, which is filled with the cream of the international neo-Nazi movements. As it is, I narrowly escaped Peter Müller—yes, your estate agent friend—as he arrived in his Ferrari ten minutes ago. I deduce it was him, after his enthusiastic greeting by the proprietors of this establishment."

174

I must have made a loud sound of protest. The odious Graham simply laughed and leant forward on the bed, thus mingling armpit with sock in a cacophony of unpleasant odours.

"You 'simply loved' the other residents of the Trois Frères I have no doubt, Dr. Hastie. So well brought-up, well-dressed, good-mannered. Am I right?"

I refused to reply. The idea that Peter Müller was at this moment in the foyer—or, worse, at my discreetly placed table in the salle à manger—was too horribly evocative of recent unpleasant experiences to do anything other than bring a sense of nausea.

"I thought you might fall for them," Graham went on with a quiet amusement which was almost intolerable, "but these people would kill you without blinking, as well as eradicate the refugee and immigrant populations of all Europe. They are the followers of Adolf Hitler. They hold your goddaughter Melissa prisoner. Is that enough for you?"

Before I could make any response, my "husband" (for I now saw he was essential to my future survival) went on to apologise and speak tenderly, a habit surely learned in those far-off days of male chauvinist superiority, when Norman Mailer and his *Time of Her Time* was considered the most telling and important description of a woman's subjugation to man.

"I'm sorry, Jean, lassie. I didna' mean to offend ye'." Graham's imitation of the Scottish accent was, needless to say,

175

atrocious. "Things being the way they are, I do believe the time has come to explain matters to you. It's not so bad to have me here, I hope. I had a bit of research to do, talked to a few old mates with their ears to the ground. Besides, as the old song has it, it's later than you think."

I settled myself on the far edge of what is, I believe, unfortunately known as a "Queen size" bed and awaited the revelations of my companion.

"You must understand that the plan of your friends, gathered here to accomplish the most historically important coup since the Norman invasion, is to bring down the euro. Am I correct, Jean, in surmising that you understand by what process this will be done? No? Relax, Dr. Hastie." (Here I must interpolate, to remark that Jim Graham's habit of instructing women to "relax" had as much of an effect, as far as I was concerned, as an injection of belladonna: I stiffened, accordingly.) "They will crash the euro by buying up the sovereign debts of the weaker states of Europe, Greece, Italy, Spain, even the UK if they feel like it. Then they will sell it fast— they will need a lot of money from somewhere—they will cause panic in all the countries of the euro-zone. The weak ones will bust, facing inconceivable poverty and social chaos; the strong, France and Germany, for example, will be faced with dumping the euro altogether and breaking up the Union. Then, in come our guys under the banner of 'Strength, Unity, and Leadership.'"

"I see," I said. That I did not understand the workings of the international money markets was not a fact I intended to pass on to Jim Graham.

At this point, Jim Graham rolled sideways on the Reveillon Rose de Nantes glazed chintz coverlet and seized my upper arm. At the same time, his pipe rolled from its resting place in the glass dish and lay smouldering on the imitation Louis XV bedside table. A black ring began to form. I squealed.

"Yes," Jim went on, his large brown eyes now not more than a few inches from my own and his breath (crumbed cod overlaid with cheap whisky) whistling straight into my face, "yes, Dr. Hastie, I do not believe that you would have tried to call Jennifer Devant, QC if you hadn't found yourself near to discovering—or remembering—the lost code."

Here, Jim Graham emitted a series of satisfied grunts at the revelation of this intelligence. The grunts revealed his extensive use of the mini-bar—located in another madly overdone article of furniture (I do not have the confidence to pronounce on its authenticity or otherwise at this stage) and were followed by stomach rumblings.

"I say, old girl, relax!" When it came to it, Graham was less of a Lothario than he liked to make out. It was his turn now to edge to the far side of the "Queen," his hand sliding down in

177

the direction of the lower stomach with a coy modesty that was distinctly surprising. We both now lay flat. I pulled myself to a sitting position, and noted with horror that my Harris Tweed skirt had ridden up above the knee and my slip, grubby from lack of laundering in this hectic time, was clearly showing.

"That's not all, Jean." Alarmed at the possible implication in Jim Graham's earnest tone I slid from the crease-resistant fabric on the bed and stood on the few inches of meanly uncarpeted tiles between the bed and the door. Surreptitiously I straightened my skirt: a repulsive smile flitted across Graham's heavy features. "I need to tell you more of the nefarious intentions of our friends the neo-Nazis downstairs. Because they'll need vast sums of cash for the purchase of the national debts."

"And so?" I enquired coldly.

"The money to which you hold the key is crucial to the whole plot. Jean, the economies of the West are ruined. Don't you see? The neo-Nazi groups are assembled here to meet in the chateau where your goddaughter Mel is already immured."

My first reaction to this was to turn and open the door from the tiny bedroom into the corridor.

Jim held up his hand to stop me. "Not so fast, Jean. I knew she was here because Lady Ray—dear Artemis—informed me of the group's plans. Incidentally, she confided to me they have her sister on the famous mad leader's cocktail—steroids, amphetamines, and the rest, guaranteed to give you the strength of a tiger though it strips away the minor stuff like common sense, judgment, and morals. More importantly, driving here, I saw Mel high in one of those mediaeval windows of the chateau. Whatever else they've done to her, the new grooming has turned the girl into a striking beauty. Had a good mind to bring her down here, enjoy a weekend together. But this is hardly the time for it, I daresay you'll agree?"

I didn't listen to the rest of Jim Graham's description of the neo-Nazi takeover of Europe. I thought only of Mel. I had known, when walking that morning in spring sunlight up the hill from the village to the chateau that she was not far from me then. I cursed myself for failing to find her, a flaxen-haired princess in a Provencal song, imprisoned behind a window high up in the walls of the castle.

"It's up to us to stop them, Dr. Hastie. And up to you to make sure they don't catch you and squeeze you till those numbers you discovered come tumbling out. That, I suppose you could say, is what I'm here for: to save you from capture and interrogation at the hands of Muller and his friends. And if you want to know how I know all this, just remember that Jim Graham still goes to the old hang-outs: the Blue Lion in Fleet Street, the Medina Bar in Cairo. . .even in Nairobi."

As the ex–Foreign Correspondent droned on, even going so far as to laughably suggest room service for the two of us, my mind raced to create a plan which would save Mel from her captors and leave my hands free to escort her home.

Graham must have noticed my silence, for he swung his legs off the bed and looked across at me. "Don't even think about making a dash for it, Jean. If necessary I'd bring you down in a rugger tackle: at least you'd be kept from the attentions of the disciples of France's Le Pen, Germany's Roeder, and British ex-aficionados of Sir Oswald Mosley et al."

Unable to prevent himself from chuckling at this further exhibition of wit, Graham energetically stuffed his pipe, and began to get it alight again. I advanced: only two steps did it. "Your idea of a room service repast sounds most tempting, Jim. Is this the menu I see on the desk under the window?"

It was. We got down to choosing the meal.

Jim Graham announced that *Steak Frites* would do the job, though he was unable to resist adding that his own *Tete de Veau Sauce Bigarade*, when made at home, was world famous.

I chose an *omelette fines herbes* and a green salad, to be followed by profiteroles.

Then we switched on the TV and watched an old movie, *All that Heaven Allows*, with subtitles in French. By the time I tiptoed round the bed, Jim Graham was noisily asleep.

PETER MÜLLER

Peter Müller and his generals met in the sparsely furnished upstairs sitting-room. Two console tables had been taken from the sides of the room and put together in the centre, with spindly gilt chairs placed around it. Only George Drago sat at the table, at its head, with a bottle and glass beside him. Lachaume sat with his legs extended in a narrow-armed chair beside the fireplace, his long face and intelligent almond eyes deliberately expressionless. Fyodor Grigoriev stood, one arm on the mantelpiece, talking to him. Toscano, in the chair opposite, tapped on his laptop. And the Dutchman, Leyden, smoked a stubby cigar, leaning against a wall near the door, looking ready to leave.

At the end of the long room Peter Müller stood by the window with his back turned to the room. He gazed over the arid landscape below, where at one time men and women might have tended vines. Once the EU agricultural policy is displaced, he thought, and once the drift to the cities is reversed, they will return. There will be peasants and small farmers again tending the land of their fathers. But, behind him, he knew something like a rebellion was growing. He turned and faced the room, taking in George Drago, whom he knew to have been the author of many massacres. Then there was Leyden, ever-angry; the cold-hearted Lachaume, whom he secretly thought of as his own Robespierre; the subtle Toscano; and the brutal Grigoriev. He respected and needed these men. Together, they would save Europe from itself and from the millions who would invade it. As he turned, Leyden burst out in English, "So where are those numbers, Muller? Have you got them? Are you hiding them from us?"

"If you'll come and sit down, I'll explain," Muller said.

Leyden marched to the table and sat down at the end opposite Drago. "Well?" he asked. Drago poured some liquid from the bottle into his glass and drank.

Muller walked rapidly from the window and took up a position in front of the fireplace. "When you hear what I have to say, you'll understand why I wanted to discuss this in a private meeting. You already know that the numbers for the secret account in Switzerland were not found in Monica Stirling's house. And that her granddaughter was never told of them."

"A pity the daughter died," Lachaume remarked, in French. Muller knew he expressed a discontent felt by all the other men in the room. The death of Monica Stirling had, he knew, been a mistake caused by the sudden intervention of a gang of neighbourhood girls, running wild on drugs, something which, in an ordered world, they would not be allowed to do. But Muller decided to explain nothing.

"There is a Scottish art historian of some kind named Jean Hastie. A childhood friend of Monica Stirling. She left a letter from Monica in the haversack that she abandoned on the train when she fled. And in this letter Monica Stirling left a clue: that Dr. Hastie has the numbers in her memory."

"Where is she now? Time is running out," Leyden said loudly.

"Shall we listen?" Lachaume said idly.

"She is on her way here," said Muller. "I have set a trap for her. She is walking into it."

"A trap!" Drago said from the table. "A stupid animal can avoid a trap. Why are we waiting?"

"I believe this Dr. Hastie is that strange woman I glimpsed at the auberge," said Toscano. "Certainly, I have never seen a woman so like a Scottish art historian in all my life. But if she is the woman we want, why is she not here? After all, the auberge is ours."

Muller said, "You are right, of course, that the woman at the auberge is Dr. Hastie. She is with an Englishman, who apparently claims to be her husband, though he is not. He is a retired journalist, a man of little repute. It would be a mistake to enter the auberge and capture her there. The woman and her companion are British and may have friends in Britain who know where they are. A violent intervention in daylight would be clumsy and dangerous. Better she comes here to find our girl, who is not only Monica's granddaughter, but also Jean Hastie's goddaughter."

"Can you be sure she'll come?"

"She is coming. My watchers at the auberge have told me. She has accomplices, an Algerian and his wife, who will be dealt with later. But first we need Dr. Hastie. We will catch her on the road here, in darkness. Or when she arrives here. Once she is in our hands, we will have those numbers. Tomorrow we will be in Switzerland to claim the money. Tomorrow, we shall begin."

"If she won't give up the numbers?" said Lachaume.

"She will give up the numbers," Drago told them.

"I think we can be sure she will," agreed Muller.

Later, Muller entered a large room on the same floor. Mel, in her elaborate red dress, sat on the edge of a huge rumpled bed, a servant at her feet, sewing the hem. As Muller entered, he heard the two of them talking. The conversation broke off as he came up. Mel, one shoulder out of her dress, said to him, "Got the pills?"

She remained very pale, but her hair had been coloured to a pale golden-brown.

Muller nodded towards the door. The servant got to her feet and left the room.

"Mel—you are very important to me—"

She held out her hand. "Come on," she said. "You said you'd bring me the pills."

"I'd prefer it if you didn't take any more. Tonight is very important. I should like you to be aware—"

"Aware of what? This is all mad—this room and that dress. Where did they dig that up from? It looks like something in a black-and-white film. Why am I here? What do you want? You told me we were going to a hotel, like a holiday. This isn't a hotel."

"I need to explain some things to you—"

"Starting with where I am. And what's going on downstairs. And I looked out of the window and there's armed coppers walking around."

Muller pulled a bottle from his pocket and found a carafe of water. He poured a glass and took it over to Mel. He shook out two tablets and gave them to her. "Lean back and relax," he said.

Mel lay back, the red dress pooling around her. Muller sat down on the side of the bed and took her hand, limp and chilly in his own. Bending towards her he said, "Mel. This is serious. You are very important to me, and to many people. You have a big part to play. You are of the blood of a conqueror, a hero. You are a symbol."

He dared not tell this ignorant girl, bred on a diet of war films and twisted history, exactly what he meant. It was too soon.

"We need you, Mel." He saw she was becoming drowsy and so he pressed his luck. "Mel—we should be together, you and I."

He had courted the girl, he had fed her drugs, he had bought her what she wanted. He knew she had been excited by him, an older man, rich and attractive, but he had never done any more than kiss her, on the cheek, or on the brow. "Together, we can do great things, greater than you can possibly imagine." But was this what she wanted to hear? "You are so pretty," he said. Then the hand withdrew from his. He took it again. This time there was resistance. She did not know what she was doing. "So pretty, and so lovely. You cannot know how much I want you."

Mel rolled to one side and put her hands over her ears. "Leave me alone."

"How can I, when you mean so much to me?" He leaned over her now. "Mel—" he said urgently. "Mel—I have waited so long."

"Please, please, please," she begged. "Please go away."

"Mel," he urged.

"Please—please—leave me alone."

He kissed her gently on the lips. She rolled further away from him and sat up, screaming, "Leave me alone! Leave me alone! I'm telling you—leave me alone! I want to go home. I want to see my Gran. I want Chris. I want to see Chris." She collapsed, face down, sobbing, mumbling, "I want to see Chris."

With effort, Muller controlled his rage. He said, "I'm sorry. I'll send the maid to you."

Whipping the door open, he found the maid too close to the door. He shook out two more pills. "She's upset," he said to her. "Give her this medicine immediately."

At the top of the stairs he met Drago, who studied his expression. "If they're not willing, a man has to make them do what he wants," said Drago. "Otherwise he's not a man at all." Muller pushed past him and went downstairs.

"Forget about the girl," Drago called after him. "The world's full of girls. It's the money we want."

JEAN HASTIE'S DIARY

I am in a laundry basket, Mr. Peter Müller's laundry basket, to be precise. It is the old-fashioned kind, I am grateful to report, made from willow, or sheep hurdles, as they are known in that part of the Borders where to "herd a hill hursel" means to bring in a flock from the Roxburghshire hills and to confine them in a pen of this same distinctly appealing plaited osier's material.

It is not easy to obtain a basket such as this, in our brash new age. I am in the back of an old van and the slats enable me to breathe more easily

Of our destination I know nothing. I am still determined to rescue my goddaughter Mel.

I have to admit that it was the egregious Jim Graham who facilitated my escape from the auberge.

Jim was finally defeated by a mille-feuilles of flaky pastry stuffed with fresh cream and confit of strawberries and topped by *fromage frais*, with a drizzle of praline sauce, and overlaid by beetroot purée. He dropped off into an uneasy slumber.

I was far from sleep. Mel was in grave danger. She must either remain with Muller to be a figurehead for the vicious men and women who planned to rule over Europe, or die. If she did not comply, they would never let her go free. I owed it to my friend Monica to save her. And now I too was threatened by these monsters.

No sensible thoughts came to me. I was trapped in this malodorous room, reverberating with the sound of my unwanted companion's snores, with no solution coming to me.

I experienced a despair which must have been akin to that of my ancestors when they suddenly realised they were predestined to eternal damnation. Suddenly, Jim stirred, flung out an arm, muttered a woman's name, "Celia" or "Cynthia," I believe, or possibly "Cynara," then sat up abruptly and remarked: "Why so pensive, fair dame?"

I explained that with my goddaughter in the hands of the cream of international Nazi groups, I did not expect to be joyful, nor was it reasonable for anyone to expect me to be. Jim, obviously one of those men who require women to be lighthearted and smiling, regardless of circumstances, was unsympathetic.

"Not much to be done about it," he declared. "The auberge is ringed with tattooed charmers you took for French workers, protecting their rights, but who are actually protecting the upper echelons of the group, like Hitler's brownshirts. The chateau where they are due to assemble is even more heavily guarded. Forgive me for pointing it out, Miss Hastie, but you are not Bruce Willis."

"Brute strength can often be overcome by intelligence," I said, although I must admit that at that moment, this was more a statement of faith than conviction.

Jim rose from the bed and began to pace, irritatingly. One of his short forays took him to the window. He stopped, peered down intently, and exclaimed: "Malek! I don't believe it."

He was out of the room in a flash. Meanwhile I went cautiously to the window and saw him approach a man in an open-necked shirt and jeans, who was loading baskets into the back of a battered white van. The two began to talk animatedly, then they exchanged embraces, and next, they went round the corner, away from the front of the building.

When Jim came upstairs again ten minutes later, he was smiling in a self-satisfied manner. "Thanks to the instincts of an old pressman, the way into the chateau is ours," he declared.

Not ours, but mine. To cut a long story short, the laundry-man was the son of the Malek with whom Jim had shared several happy days and nights holed up in a cave during the late war of independence in Algeria.

"I was just a lad at the outset of my career," he told me. "Learning the noble art of lying flat while the bullets fly around you, while you, no doubt were hanging around the Deux Magots with the rest of the armchair soldiers."

These flashes of perception from Jim, whose brain has otherwise been pickled by a combination of alcohol and libido, never cease to surprise. "While you were talking about being and essence or essence and being, old Malek and I were sitting on bare earth sharing our last drops of water, stuck between two armies."

Jim's new friend knocked on the door, slid inside, greeted me politely, and offered to drive us hidden inside his van to the chateau. Since he was the regular laundryman, he would be allowed inside without question. Truly a piece of good fortune at a very dark time. And the credit for it must go to Jim.

It seemed best to me that Jim should remain at the auberge while I went alone up to the chateau. I appealed to him to remain, saying that, if present, he would increase our chances of detection, while if he remained at the auberge he would be an invaluable conduit for information and contacts with the authorities. I was acutely aware that matters might go badly awry and that intervention by the local police, the British Embassy, or even, God forbid, the press, might be the only help.

"These people are very dangerous," Jim warned.

"I am fully aware of that. They have killed my friend, they have killed an innocent young man, and they have abducted my goddaughter," was my frigid response to this obvious statement.

My tweed suit was lying desolate on the bed and I was clad in a long patterned skirt and a patterned blouse. Malek's wife tied on a headscarf which concealed my hair and brow. She secured it under my chin. I looked at myself doubtfully in the mirror. My face was too pale, my eyes too blue.

"It's not very convincing," I said.

Jim snorted. "They won't look at you," he said.

Malek's wife was more polite: "They don't look at the servants, especially us."

"I could get used to it, though," Jim offered, with what I can only describe as a leer, although this expression quickly left his face when he saw mine. "I mean, it's more feminine, somehow," he added weakly. I did not reply.

Inevitably, there was further argument about the plan. Jim did not want me to face the ordeal alone. I reiterated that his presence in the van would further endanger us and that he would be more useful at the auberge. I discovered that in times of crisis there is seldom time for lengthy debate: decisions must be made quickly, even if they later turn out to have been wrong. Malek and his wife descended the staircase with suitable bundles of linen and I followed, my head bent, carrying a pile of pillows. As I left the room, I had time to say to Jim: "I am worried about Malek and Nassima."

"They know what those people stand for," he said. "What do you think will happen to them if Muller and his gang take over?"

Algerians in France are chiefly housed in what are known as the "banlieues," which are not the leafy suburbs suggested by the word, but vast housing estates where the residents are easy to find and therefore easy to control, like the ghettoes where other European immigrants once lived.

A chilling thought to carry with me as I hurried after Malek and Nassima.

I walked down the corridor of the *Trois Frères*, turned down the staircase and walked, stooped, past the desk, past the assorted evil-doers sipping after-dinner coffee in salon and dining-room, swinging their Gucci-clad feet and planning their next attack, suitably attired in Versace and Givenchy.

Now, crouched in clothing belonging to Muller and his servants, I am reduced to the status of those very poor and unwanted the neo-Nazis wish to see eliminated from the face of the world.

For, not to put too fine a point on it, I was forced to accommodate myself in this basket.

THE DISGUISE OF JEAN HASTIE

I am alone, standing on the side of the hill.

The stars are bright, as bright as the pinpoints of light that entered my willow basket through the holes in the plaiting.

When the car stopped suddenly, there were footsteps, the back of the van was flung open and Malek's voice was raised in protest: "There's nothing in there but laundry."

I could only conclude that this was a roadblock, an additional precaution due to the status of the expected guests and the importance of their deliberations. If I were found, I would be a dead woman, and if I refused to give Muller and his associates the numbers to the secret account, they would torture me until I did. Muller had been unable to find the numbers in Monica's house, Muller would know by now that Mel had never been entrusted with them, and therefore the only person in the world who knew those numbers was I, Jean Hastie. This information I had not fully confided to Jim, anticipating that were I to tell him he would immediately come up with some rash scheme which would make this already dreadful situation worse.

Meanwhile Malek had started an argument with someone, presumably one of the guards manning the roadblock, protesting that he had a pass to get into the chateau and had never been stopped before.

Then I heard retreating feet and a third voice. Malek had decoyed the searchers away from me to the front of the van. My safety, and his, depended on my leaving the vehicle speedily, and undetected.

I pushed up the lid of the hamper in which I lay and crawled out, while at the front of the van the dispute continued. On hands and knees, I crawled to the door, then I pushed myself out onto the road and fell down into the darkness and took one of the baskets with me to aid my disguise.

A fine situation, indeed, for a woman with excellent qualifications and a prominent member of the Board of the Scottish National Trust, lying bruised and scraped on a dark road in the French countryside, disguised in a long skirt and headscarf.

But much was at stake: Mel's well-being, possibly her life, and the future of Hitler's foul fortune and the foul uses to which it would be put if it fell into the wrong hands.

While Malek continued to argue, and the guards became more abusive to him, I got to my feet and ran uphill. Casting a look backwards, I observed one of the guards. To him I was now a woman, in crumpled Arab dress, and I guessed that to the others I would seem very much the same, stained and fatigued after a long walk in the scrub. I had been a stowaway in a van— they would understand that.

Suddenly I found myself encircled by small, dirty, and irritating children, swarthy as young Heathcliff when he was picked up on the streets of Liverpool. I asked the brats where I could find a telephone. We stood a little way up a gentle incline, and it should have been satisfying to witness the neo-Nazis sweeping by, unaware that Jean Hastie, their arch enemy, watched them, ready to deprive them of the kingdom so closely within their reach.

There was no telephone. I made a signal suggestive of a mobile (I loathe them) but this was misinterpreted, and met with howls of laughter.

I trudged down the road in search of some sign of civilisation.

Finally, I came to a small village. Here was a bar, indeed: my spirits rose accordingly, and, without realising the sight I presented to the world, I went inside.

The astonishment and rage at my effrontery was violent; certainly I shall never forget my reception in the neat and pleasant little village not two kilometres from Gordes. In excellent French, I asked if I might use a telephone.

First, menacing laughter. Laughter so dangerous, so threatening, that I had no choice but to turn around, and, still lugging my basket, go trembling out into the night.

I knew what it was, on that terrible day, to be an immigrant in the brave new Europe.

I ran on. A half moon looks down uncertainly. The stars are still bright.

My legs found the track and followed it, always upwards. A dog barks. Then I hear an anthem—music—it takes me back to school, to the songs I was taught with Monica, to the map of Europe, most of it red and impenetrable, on the wall of the shabby little schoolhouse at Edleston.

Suddenly, a pair of gates rear up like heraldic beasts across the road—no longer a track, smartly tarmacked, wider, curving between watered lawns green in the spotlights.

A man sits by the gates. A security guard. He nods at me and waves me through.

I am the Arab servant woman—the hood of my robe is close round my head. I walk through, my eyes on the ground, every bone in my body as servile as I can make it.

I reach the bend in the road which leads to the front lawn. Between two large spotlights I see a dark patch of grass, like a blemish on a face. I run to it. I crouch. The French windows of the house are straight ahead of me. I look in.

The dinner party in progress takes place in a room strangely reminiscent of one of those period dramas—Merchant and Ivory, possibly, or *Brideshead*—with chandelier, napiery, pale portraits on eau-de-Nil silk walls in imitation of thirties decor. The dining-table, maplewood, and the chairs, replica Chippendale, are all of a kind that an industrialist might have liked for his Provencal home.

The guests, inevitably, are clothed in white ties, also very dated in appearance, with the ladies in strapless ball gowns, crimped hair, and antiquated jewellery: Cartier, Duchess of Windsor tigers, sapphire-eyed parrots on diamond-encrusted mounts (I must add here that I dislike this era more than any and am far from surprised it took a second World War to put an end to such posturing and ugliness).

It is all a masquerade of the most unpleasant kind. Among the guests, there are those who, because of their age, are no doubt looking back nostalgically to their youth in the days of the undefeated Third Reich, and looking forward, no doubt, to its revival. But there are many younger faces present, set in lines of power and greed above the black ties and white shirtfronts.

Beside them are their consorts, almost all blonde, whether naturally or artificially, well coiffed, finely clad, bedecked in jewellery, women who do not know, or care, what the men do, so long as there are yachts and jewels aplenty. Black-clad

199

manservants circulate with champagne; there is a buzz of conversation and laughter. It might any party for the rich, anywhere, were it not for the fact that behind each man's chair stands a thug in a black tee shirt and jeans, and at each door stands a guard in a black kevlar vest, holding the kind of gun seen on posters for Hollywood action films.

It is unusual, to say the least, for one such as myself, a conserver of ancient buildings and an expert on the arts and antiquities of my native land, to be found kneeling on dry grass in a landscape of execrable taste while looking in at a collection of monstrous fakes and forgeries. I recognise a prominent Russian politician. On either side of the Russian politician are two women: artificial hair, yellow as dead corn, flows over their shoulders in braids, like a picture of Rhine maidens in Germany, circa 1937.

At the head of the table are two empty chairs and I dread to think for whom they are intended.

To my horror, in comes Muller with Mel on his arm. He is in black, of course. She is in a red taffeta dress, low cut, with blood-red stones in her ears and at her throat. Her face is painted very white and to my inexpert eyes she seems drugged.

Muller pulls out one of the chairs at the head of the table and puts her in it. She hardly knows where she is or what she is doing. And then, horrors, a servant comes up to him with a message and Muller bends down and says something to her in a low voice and walks away from the table, through the French doors, and past me. A second man joins him and they begin to speak.

The spotlight has begun to move—and I must move too. Even if I have to kneel on the flagstones, painfully hard when only a flimsy skirt separates them from a swollen knee joint sadly afflicted with arthritis, the unpleasant necessity forces me closer to the house. And now, before I have time to bemoan the loss of my protective Harris Tweed skirt, I find I am only inches from the glass door leading to the dining-room. Worse still. I am on hands and knees and see only the high polish of black shoes (Lobb of St James's). Two men have opened the glass door and stepped out into the evening air.

They say the natural world can on occasion come to the rescue, in circumstances as unprecedented as mine. Or, in return for a kind deed performed in the past, the grateful member of another species will throw an obstacle in the enemy path. I saw a scorpion—black, unmistakable in form. We stayed there, not moving, as the shoes of Peter Müller and his Russian guest came up to us and paused.

I must confess here that Providence—or fate or destiny, whatever we may like to call those forces which sometimes side with us (though most often they do not)—gave magnificently with both hands. For, while thanking our Lord for the scorpion's static pose (had it scuttled, as I believe may be the term, into the ill-fitting skirt and thence to the brassière, a solid construction of wire and polyester from Jenner's in Edinburgh, the outcome would have been dreadful indeed)—while giving thanks to God, as I say, Peter Müller bent down and removed his left shoe. He ran a finger round its interior, as if trying to dislodge a pebble. Then he gazed at the ground and his eyes swept sideways, and he saw me there.

I was seen: but I was not seen. Like the women who crawl aboard the great jets as they come down in Karachi or Bangkok, I was no more than a cleaner who picks the discarded trifles of the West from the cabin floor. Muller hopped on one foot, caught shoeless by what was clearly a challenging question. And I? As he spoke and hopped, I placed the friendly scorpion deep in his waiting shoe. There it lay patiently. What had I done, what wasp or motorway frog had I saved, to deserve this extraordinary piece of fortune?

With the two men still muttering their questions and answers outside, inside the dining-room, the neo-Nazis all hold champagne glasses and raise them in a toast towards the dim figure in the garden, their host, Peter Müller. The glass door has been left open: I am still invisible, both in shadow and metaphorically; an Arab woman who sweeps the terraces of the rich and powerful. Inside, I see Mel. Her dress, with its chiffon sleeves and red organza bell shape, is less of a period creation than the dresses worn by the other women. Her hands in elbow-length white gloves—these seem to be *de rigueur* with all the ladies—rise and flutter as she drains her glass and replaces it on the table. Something amuses her. The anthem swells out once more.

My eyes are on the woman they now all toast, the young woman, surely my goddaughter Mel, my poor misguided Mel. But as she turns, the expression on her face is suddenly desolate and desolating. Is it because she does not know what she is doing here, or is it because she does?

Clemency Wilsford, on the far side of the President, I recognise still from all the newspaper articles, the silly films "investigating" her love affair with Adolf Hitler, the rumours of St Ronan's House occupied by her despite the most valiant efforts of the Trust.

Clemency Wilsford, with her sinister, drug-induced youth, her wig of golden curls, her blue eyes like drained pools, stares out at me.

Let boldness be my friend. I walk into the room and straight to the head of the table and I whisper into Mel's ear, "I am Jean Hastie, your godmother. You are in danger. Come with me." What she will do at that moment is uncertain. She is drugged and therefore in a condition where the rational mind is stilled. But whether she will come with me, or stand and denounce me, or simply lean back witlessly in her chair hangs on what she feels at that moment about her situation. And, mercifully, I am correct in thinking her unhappy, for she rises, without any apparent reaction, and together we leave the room through the back, where the guard has temporarily moved aside to allow passage into the room to two servants, trays held high. After all, we have not been followed, there is no disturbance, the guests at the table have made no outcry, evidently unsurprised to see their totem, their figurehead, the drugged bride of the monster they are trying to create, leaving the room with an Arab woman, a servant perhaps, with pins, a jewelled haircomb, a pair of gloves.

But I am aware we have only moments. I draw Mel down a wide, tiled passageway where pale, cold statuary stands in niches. Using a full-sized marble statue of a muscular Greek or Roman hero as cover I push Mel into the gap in front of a bare torso, a knee and a large foot treading down some mythical beast, and, exposing myself to anyone who might come from the dining-room, tell her urgently: "It was the man you are with, Peter Müller, who killed your grandmother. He needs you and when he does not, he may kill you, too. Please believe me." I spare her the knowledge of Chris's death and there is too little time to explain the business of the numbers to that account containing gold wrenched from the hands of the dead.

One of Mel's hands is on the wall beside the statue, supporting her. She looks at me with eyes in which understanding comes and goes like clouds scudding across a sky. Her response is agonisingly slow to come.

"He's crazy. He hit on me when I was dressing for the party. He killed Monica?"

I fail to understand. "Hit you?"

"His hands were all over me. He kept mumbling and muttering about marrying me and making us emperors. I didn't know what he was on."

"He was on power, the most potent drug of all. Mel—we must get away." I pull at her arm but she resists.

"What about my Gran? He killed her? Peter?" An aggressive light comes into her eyes. "I'll kill him, the bastard," and she begins to pull away from me, as if to rush back down the corridor, dart into a room full of enemies, find Muller and attack him.

I think of the scorpion in Muller's shoe and wonder briefly what that scorpion thinks he's doing—not, apparently, what scorpions are famous for—and then say to Mel, urgently, "That can wait. They will kill you, Mel, if you defy them. Me, too, if you care about that. Monica would not want you dead."

All hinged now on Mel's decision which, almost like an ordinary teenager in an ordinary situation, she did not impart to me. Instead she wrenches away, plucks up her long red skirt, and runs off down the corridor, fleet as a hare, with me in effortful pursuit. She passes the open door of the dining-room, glimpsing the guests.

Mel is by now through another door and out into the garden but I know Muller was there less than ten minutes earlier, and may still be. If he sees her, we are both lost, and it will not be long, anyway, before the guests understand Mel is running, and know she must be caught.

Muller is still there, on the terrace, and he and his companion have been joined by a third man. They are concluding their conversation. Muller is putting his foot into his shoe when Mel flashes past in her red dress, hair flying. Muller shouts—and at that moment I trip and fall, winded—trapped.

I get to my knees, slowly, knowing it doesn't matter any more. We are defeated. I can already hear guests coming from the dining-room, alarmed. I am about to be caught here, and Mel will be captured by the guards at the gate. I have failed; my struggle is over.

The patch of deep shadow where I kneel moves and trembles as a sudden wind blows a branch of an umbrella pine across the relentless white beam of a spotlight.

Then comes the scream. It rises, high and desperate, and ends with a choking, throttled sound that brings Peter Müller to his knees (and I could swear his wild, bloodshot eyes, distended in the agony of the scorpion's sting, looked straight out at me). Everyone jumps to their feet. A security guard pulls a gun and shoots, shattering the glass door.

I rise. I go as slowly as I can, and with the steps of a woman wanted only for the menial tasks she will perform. I find Mel at the edge of the lawn, looking back on the chaotic scene behind us. I take her hand and lead her out over the broken glass and to the back of the villa. Here, a row of parked cars, a sleeping chauffeur. . .

I, Jean Hastie, would prefer not to remember my drive in the stolen Citroen to Nice airport, on a corniche that seems nowadays to be all motorway and not to resemble in the slightest the dashing drives taken by Grace Kelly in Hitchcock's *To Catch a Thief*.

But then again, Jim Graham is no Cary Grant.

There is a lot of time to make up, with Mel. On the plane to Heathrow I had to tell her about Chris's death. She was greatly upset. It was a sober couple who found Jennifer Devant's placard with "Hastie" held high in Arrivals.

One day, when Mel is cleared of the crime I am convinced she did not commit, we can go into the past together. I can teach the child some of the history she so sadly lacks.

207

Jim Graham said he had put a stop to matters by calling the French and then International Police several times. "It would have helped, Jean, if you could have found the time to do this," he said, and had the impertinence to sound aggrieved.

I give him credit for having made alarmist calls to the authorities, but initially the authorities took little interest in the supposed abduction in London of a fifteen-year-old girl, never reported to the British police. However, Jim's garbled and near-incredible tale of the abduction and the massing of far-right forces at the chateau (and he claims, the very mention of his name) did have some effect. The house was raided by the police on the following morning but by then—perhaps tipped off by sympathisers—the guests, no strangers to trouble, one assumes, had quickly packed their bags and gone, with the speed of ants when the anthill is kicked over. Jim was at the window as they left before dawn, sweeping through the village in a convoy of limousines; the motorcade, he said, would have put the President of the United States to shame. Presumably the body of Muller went with them, for it was not found at the chateau, and must now lie in whatever unmarked grave, in whatever country, his associates could find for him.

By the time we had arrived in the city centre, Jennifer had taken pity on my state of exhaustion. She assured me I was at liberty to stay at the Avondale Club for the night and, even better, borrow her second-best suit. "Tweed. I had it made in Peebles," Jennifer Devant, QC announced, as Mel simply giggled, and, worryingly, I thought, asked "Uncle Jim" if she could go to his house in Banesbury Road. However, I have decided to leave well alone. By now the villa in the Luberon mountains will have been surrounded by police and armed forces, and Peter Miller of Miller, Brown & Co. will no longer be known in North West London—or anywhere else—as a friendly neighbourhood estate agent. This at least was worth accomplishing, in the search for the killer of Monica Stirling.

And as for Hitler's gold: Jennifer advises me strongly that until some better plan is made for it, I had better not mention that I alone have the secret of the numbers which will release it.

JEAN HASTIE'S DIARY

I am enjoying my retirement, and, I must own, my second cup of coffee of the morning, while awaiting the results of our General Election.

Will the same Government, thought satisfactory by some, considered as betrayers of the Welfare State by others, be returned to power? Or have we seen the last of them, to find ourselves once more in uncharted, and possibly menacing, waters?

Speculation is of course pointless. My friend Jennifer Devant, who has just returned from a long and lucrative spell in Washington, says:

"If Peter Müller hadn't been killed, I do believe he would have wriggled free in France, and somehow have brought together his 'pan-European' movement, as he had planned. We have reason to thank the scorpion, and of course yourself," she adds. "How on earth did you persuade the British police to lay off Melissa Stirling and go for Muller. Too late, of course, as usual."

"Simple, Dame Jennifer," I replied. "I watched the video of the attack on poor Monica very thoroughly."

"Indeed, we all did," came the rejoinder, as I had known it would.

"The hand which held the knife that killed Monica," I said, "was attached to an arm, would you not say?"

"My dear Baroness Hastie, have you taken leave of your senses? Obviously the hand was attached to an arm."

"Good. I am glad you agree. The arm was white, wasn't it?"

"Well, yes."

"Do not imagine that I stray into political territory inhabited by Herr Muller and his friends," I said. "I would simply like to point out that every single member of the group which came down the road and fell on poor Monica was tattooed on practically every inch of the body, certainly on the arms."

"So?" said Jennifer Devant for the first time in her life, looking suitably mystified.

"So Peter Miller, masquerading as the neighbourhood estate agent, glimpsed one moment at the end of the road, was next in the group—every one of whom was dependent on him for feeding a carefully nurtured drug habit—and holding the knife brought to the site for the purpose of killing Monica after finding the secret code number."

"Peter Miller," said Jennifer Devant. "You know, I did think in that video that the arm and hand were more like the limb of a man than a woman's could be."

"You didn't say so at the time," I said. "Nor was this noted by our valiant investigative reporter James Graham, despite the many times, I have no doubt, he must have watched the video, to feed his passion for an underage girl."

"Yes, yes," said Jennifer quickly. She does not appear to like my comments on the subject of the marriage of Jim Graham and Melissa Stirling. "But they're happy now, Jean, aren't they?"

I informed my friend that I had little information on the couple. They had left Banesbury Road some years back, and no-one appeared to know their whereabouts, despite rumours they had settled in Argentina or Brazil.

"Dear Mel," said Jennifer Devant, extracting a small black cheroot from her bag and lighting up.

"Melissa's manners have not improved," I said sharply. "My last Christmas card, hand-painted I have to say, went unacknowledged. A goddaughter has responsibilities towards her godmother, after a certain age."

"But where did you send it, Jean?" Jennifer looks at me through a cloud of devilish black smoke as she so often does, this time to the accompaniment of cheering from the TV on the occasion of another far-right candidate sweeping in as Member for Parliament.

I rose to go and rinse my coffee cup, an action which I find is lamentably seldom performed in the grand country houses I still visit as retired President of the Scottish National Trust. "I send the cards every Christmas, care of Artemis Lady Ray, at Amesbury House," I told Jennifer. "There is no excuse whatsoever in Mel's failure to reply."

"Lady Ray?" Jennifer looks astonished. "Surely, Jean, she would hardly know where the girl has gone?"

It is true, as I reflected later, that I omitted to inform the world-famous barrister of the gift to me made by Clemency Wilsford's sister of the journals kept by the misguided girl during her years in Berlin, then at St Ronan's.

"I disagree," I said, aware of sounding pompous. "Mel is Lady Ray's great-niece after all."

"Are you saying, then, that blood is thicker than water?" counters Dame Jennifer Devant. A glint has entered her eye and the cheroot is waved imperiously.

"Maybe," I reply.